LADY ARABELLA AND THE BARON
THE SEDGEWICK LADIES
BOOK I

ISABELLA THORNE

Mikita Associates

PART I

CHAPTER 1

Lady Arabella Sedgewick, the eldest daughter of the Earl of Ashbury, tossed a letter disdainfully onto the glossy writing desk, barely resisting the impulse to crumple the costly, delicate parchment. The pages scattered, mingling with previously discarded correspondence. She stalked momentarily away from the mess to stare blindly out of her chamber window where the trees of her father's estate grew lush and green. She brushed back a blonde strand of hair which had divested itself from the pins and uncurled from the complicated updo that her maid had labored to create. She tucked the errant lock carefully behind her ear, hoping she didn't look untidy. Her hair, straight as a pin, often divested itself from every fastening her maid tried, much to Arabella's dismay.

The estate below bustled with activity; the grounds perfectly manicured, but her father, the Earl of Ashbury, was nowhere in sight. Arabella knew that Wilkins, the head gardener, had most likely worked his fingers to the bone in order to have everything presented so flawlessly, with as little notice as the Sedgewicks had given of their return home. The roses were in full bloom this late in the summer and were lovely enough to make even the Dowager Mayberry green with envy. The scent of them wafted to Arabella on a light breeze, and she closed her eyes in bliss. The breeze felt heavenly. How could she possibly be discontented in such lovely surroundings?

The lawns were trimmed to perfection, and as far as the eye could see, the lands of the Earl of Ashbury spread out in pastoral beauty. To the north, via the North Road, was the town of Northwickshire and to the south was the village of Knoxington, about an hour's ride by carriage, less on horseback. Further south, of course, was London. Arabella breathed deeply as a summer breeze again picked up a few stray blonde strands and continued to destroy her maid's work. The respite was welcome. Lady Arabella was monumentally glad to be home. No one here in the country gave her appearance any mind. No one here cared if she acted the lady, although such actions were not really an inconvenience. She enjoyed being in charge of her father's household. It was a burden she had taken on as a young girl when her mother passed, but there were certain responsibilities as a member of the Ton. Certain niceties were to be expected.

Really, they ought to have remained in Bath another fortnight, at the least. The little season in Bath was not over, but when Lord Ashbury announced his desire to cut short his family's holiday, it occurred to no one except his youngest daughter Daphne to voice an objection, and he had summarily ignored her protests. Privately, Arabella thought that his gout had flared up, as evidenced by his notice to the doctor once they arrived home.

When Arabella suggested this to her younger sister, Daphne, in the hopes that the girl would have some compassion for their father, the girl exploded with frustration and threw up her hands in exasperation.

"It's Bath," she cried, voicing an expletive that had Arabella raise her eyebrows. "The whole reason to go there is to take the waters and be cured! I don't know why he couldn't soak his toe," she muttered in a pique.

"Surely not the whole reason to go to Bath," said Arabella, thinking of the continual round of balls, soirées, and suitors, but Daphne stomped from the room undeterred in her ire.

Arabella, as the Earl of Ashbury's eldest child, might have been expected to have some influence over her father, but she did not complain. Daphne had certainly seemed to consider her a traitor for not sharing her outrage at the truncated holiday, but Arabella rarely ventured to say anything that might displease Lord Ashbury. She never wanted to add to the burden of sorrow that her father had carried ever since the untimely death of his wife eight years ago. Besides, Arabella was heartily sick of Bath and had been well enough pleased to return to the Sedgewick family's country estate, although the trip home from Bath was long, hot, and tedious.

Turning away from the window to pace the length of her chamber, Arabella fought against the growing sense of agitation that threatened to well up within her breast. It had been a foolish, childish hope; the idea that she might fall in love that summer. She sighed. She wasn't going to waste any more time on such romantic nonsense. There had been suitors a-plenty in Bath, just as there had been in London for the last two Seasons, and each and every one of them had left her utterly indifferent.

"Goodness, did someone sneak into your chamber and disorder your correspondence?" Marianne, the middle Sedgewick daughter, asked laughingly from the doorway, startling Arabella. "I don't think I've seen such a mess dare come anywhere near you since you were ten-years-old."

"Don't be ridiculous," Arabella replied, flushing with annoyance as she hurried to gather up the scattered papers. Arabella was fastidiously neat, and Marianne, who was more of a free spirit, constantly teased her about her obsessive tidiness. Arabella loved Marianne, but she had wanted to take just a few brief moments for herself, without having to play the role of the cool and composed eldest daughter, even if it was a role that Marianne generally saw through with disconcerting accuracy.

"I was only teasing. You do know it isn't exactly a cardinal sin to have a few papers strewn about, don't you?" Marianne said as she entered her sister's room. "In fact, you could blame it on the wind," her sister suggested as another errant breeze ruffled some of the papers, making the piles more askew. "Are they all letters from your many admirers?" Marianne continued as she caught up a page at random and lifted one eyebrow at the contents. "This gentleman certainly seems to be of the opinion that you are *perfection incarnate*," she quoted.

"That must be from Lord Hilliard's last letter, I'm missing a page or two," Arabella said, taking back her correspondence and fixing it into a neat stack. She searched for the missing pages which had fallen beneath the bed. "Ah! Here they are," she said triumphantly.

"No, it's not from Hilliard. It's signed Yours Eternally, Sir Giles Fenwick," Marianne replied.

"Oh well, they all sound precisely the same, don't they? That's the whole problem." Arabella gave up the pretense of composure and smoothed her dress so as to not wrinkle it. She sat down with a disgusted sigh. "How on earth am I supposed to choose a suitable match when I can't even tell one gentleman's letter from the next? There has to be something wrong with me, Marianne," she said as she attempted to re-pin the errant strand of hair that fell over her cheek. "I simply cannot seem to feel *anything* for any of them."

"I wouldn't judge yourself too harshly on that point, dearest," Marianne soothed as she pinned her older sister's hair for her. Marianne was also blonde, but her hair stayed obediently in neatly restrained curls.

"Thank you," Arabella said, feeling much more settled now that her hair was in place.

Marianne paced across the room and looked through the pile of correspondence. "Several of these letters look to be copied from the same collection of *Model Correspondence for Young Gentlemen*, unless I am very much mistaken."

"You made that up. There isn't any such book." Although, if there were such a book, Marianne would surely know of it. Arabella smiled in spite of herself.

"Oh, I daresay there is, or something very like it," Marianne said sitting beside her sister on the bed. "Even if there isn't, no one could blame you for being unmoved by such bland love letters as these." She waved the offending piece of parchment above her head. "My question is, why are you in such a rush all of a sudden to make some unimaginative gentleman's most predictable dreams come true?"

"It's foolish; I'd really rather not say," hedged Arabella, nipping sheets of parchment out of her sister's grasp in a futile attempt at distraction. She straightened them, precisely matching the corners.

"You'd really rather I go away and leave you to compose yourself, too," Marianne laughed. "You forget, I'm one of the few people in this wide world who knows that you aren't nearly so icy as you choose to appear. And as such, you must know I am wrung out from the trip north."

"It was uncomfortably hot in the coach, was it not?" Arabella agreed.

"You shan't get rid of me by talking about the weather," Marianne pronounced. "I know you. You are vexed with the monotony of the suitors, but you are also bored to tears with inactivity; therefore, you'll have a terribly difficult time getting rid of me at present, so you may as well have out with it." Her sister shrugged with feigned nonchalance.

"Very well, have it your own way, then. I had hoped, foolishly, as it turns out, to meet *someone* this summer who might inspire my regard. Since I most decidedly did not, and since I have absolutely no desire to endure another Season in London, I have concluded that I must encourage one of these—" She waved a letter about distractedly and turned up her nose.

"Insipid fops? Vapid swains?" suggested Marianne helpfully when Arabella trailed off. "Vapid swains?"

"Ardent suitors," Arabella corrected with a frown. "And you aren't nearly so amusing or helpful as you seem to believe."

"I am marvelously amusing, I assure you," said Marianne with a toss of her strawberry blonde curls. "And as for helpful, why on earth would I help you to marry any of these imbeciles? In this particular case, it is my duty as your sister to be as *un*helpful as possible."

"It is my duty as *your* sister to make a good match with all due haste, so that you and Daphne can be out, unhindered by an unmarried eldest sister who is nearly a spinster."

"Oh posh. You are no spinster at age nineteen."

"Nearly twenty," Arabella broke in as she stood to straighten the mess of correspondence.

"Ah, yes. There's a grand age," Marianne teased. "And don't use either Daphne or myself as an excuse for this folly," Marianne protested, her lighthearted, teasing manner dropping away suddenly. "Daphne is scarcely more than a child, without the slightest notion of coming out. She would much rather muck about in the stable as settle to be fitted for a ball gown. As for myself, I cannot claim any impatience to participate in the coming Season. If I did, however, no one would object in the slightest to two sisters being out at once. Why, even our Great Aunt Myrtle isn't so old-fashioned as that!"

"All the same, people *do* talk if a younger sister is engaged or wed before the eldest," Arabella said stubbornly. "I won't do anything to bring even a whiff of gossip upon our family, you know that."

"And you think there is even the slightest chance that I will make a match before you?" Marianne arched a brow at her older sister, who was generally acknowledged to be the beauty of not only the family, but of their entire connection, although Arabella would not say it was so. She purported that her nose was too long and her hair was too straight. She much preferred her sister's riotous curls over her own lackluster straight blonde hair.

"Shall I fetch you a looking-glass?" Marianne asked. "Or perhaps we can sift through these letters and find a few of the odes to *your hair like satin or voice of an angel* or your *eyes the color of a summer sky*, and don't get me started on your *porcelain or is it rose-petal skin*?"

"Nonsense," Arabella impatiently brushed Marianne's words away. Far from being vain about her looks, she had always harbored a secret fear that she had inherited their mother's reckless and impulsive spirit, along with her pure platinum blonde hair and blue eyes. Besides, she hated for Marianne or anyone else to make comparisons. "You are twice the beauty I could ever be, especially when you can be bothered to remember to spend more than five minutes on your appearance. And anyway, that is all beside the point. I am nearly twenty years of age, and it is high time I made a match. I need to make this decision and be done with it."

"Arabella, the problem is, once you make this decision, you are most certainly not *done with it*. I mean, you will not be done with the man. He will be a part of your life for the rest of your life."

Arabella sighed. "Don't remind me," she muttered.

"If you were even the slightest bit excited by that prospect, Arabella, to say nothing of joyful, I would hardly feel so concerned, but you cannot expect me to encourage you in anything that makes you look so utterly miserable."

"I'm not miserable. I was simply taking a moment to set aside some foolish fancies I had been cherishing—a *private* moment, I might add. Any of these gentlemen would make excellent husbands, I am sure," she said, picking up two of the letters and perusing them. "It's simply a matter of deciding which one to encourage."

"That seems terribly cold," Marianne murmured, putting an arm around her sister and resting her reddish-gold head on Arabella's shoulder to take any sting out of the observation.

"No, it's merely logical. I don't wish to participate in another Season, or to be a burden of any sort to my family, and I have proven to myself that I do not have the type of nature that falls madly in love. If, indeed, falling in love even exists outside of novels. The logical conclusion, then, is to encourage the most suitable of my admirers without any further prevarication."

"I suppose it has taken a great deal of prevarication to keep all of these suitors at an arm's length without actually dashing their hopes," conceded Marianne, knowing from her sister's stubborn tone that any further argument would only serve to further entrench her opinion.

"An exhausting amount, really," Arabella admitted. "It will be a relief, if I could just make up my mind once and for all," Arabella assured her with a brief hug. "But I will never manage that if I can't have a few minutes of solitude, and you know we are going to be inundated with callers as soon as word gets out that we've returned home early."

"I hope you'll take more than a few minutes to make such a monumental decision," Marianne couldn't keep from saying disapprovingly. "But I will certainly leave you to it."

Arabella attempted to resume her tasks, but was soon forced to admit defeat, at least temporarily. Marianne's evident disapproval left her questioning her judgment, an annoyance since she had spent the entire journey home coming to her decision to choose a suitor and had no desire to revisit the question. It was very like Marianne, she reflected, to question the basic and unstated rules of society and knock her logic all askew. Marianne had a stubborn streak of whimsy that, combined with a keen intellect, had her always wondering *why* things had to be a certain way.

They had all coped with the loss of Lady Ashbury in their own ways, Arabella reflected, gathering up the scattered letters one last time and sorting them into orderly piles to be analyzed later. Her father's grief had manifested itself in a retreat from seemingly all emotions; Marianne had delved into books in a constant quest to understand everything, and Daphne's grief came forth in a fiery and willful manner that was often termed spoiled.

The thought made Arabella defensive, as always. Daphne was far from spoiled. The girl was generous and warm-hearted, with no tolerance for any perceived injustice. If she was a little headstrong, well, such could be expected from a girl who had lost her mother at such a young age, after all. Arabella and Marianne had done their best to nurture and guide poor little Daphne, but as they had been children themselves, reeling with shock and sorrow, their best had perhaps not been quite good enough. *That* idea stung particularly, as Arabella acknowledged that her own particular manner of coping had been to attempt absolute perfection in all things. Perhaps such a goal was unattainable, but that had never stopped her from striving for it.

With a sigh, she set aside the uninspiring missives from her suitors. They might seem more appealing in the morning, but even if they did not, she would proceed with her plan. Perhaps she might summon a little more interest if she made a list of ideal qualifications, she thought, only she would leave off any silly, romantic notions. It was all too plain that she would not find a man who could make her heart skip a beat or make her smile or sing just by thinking of him. Not a single one of the gentlemen that she had been paraded before in the past two years had even come close to such an accomplishment. She was quite sure her perfect gentleman did not exist, except perhaps in one of Marianne's novels.

CHAPTER 2

Arabella suppressed a small sigh as she allowed Mr. Potts to seat her at the silent breakfast table. Lord Ashbury did not stand as the ladies entered the room. He was frowning over his papers as he ate, apparently oblivious to the presence of anyone else. His foot was elevated on a small footstool, giving credence to Arabella's guess that his gout brought them home early.

"Thank you, Mr. Potts," she said. "What did the doctor say about your gout?" Arabella ventured, but Father barely looked up from his paper as he snorted.

"Young pup, Larkin, doesn't know a thing about doctoring. He wouldn't give me any powders at all. Said my eating was to blame. No honey cakes or sugar biscuits, no liver pate or kidney pie, and no brandy," Father added as if that were the last straw. He sniffed at the thought. "Larkin said I should eat more cabbage and turnips. Peasant food. I tell you, the man's daft." Her father harrumphed as the footman brought a fresh hot pot of tea to the table.

Arabella took a sip of her tea and noted that her father did not load his plate with sweet biscuits, as per his usual fare, but instead, his plate held a generous portion of eggs, and he took his tea black. She smiled slightly into her cup.

Daphne was still sulking in protest of their early return home from Bath, a charming scowl creasing her sweet face. She hadn't taken a bite of breakfast. Arabella suspected Daphne had practiced the mournful expression in the mirror in order to still look so remarkably pretty while pouting. At fourteen, the child was certainly already aware of her own beauty, Arabella thought as she placed her napkin on her lap.

"You'll give yourself a headache if you keep frowning so hard, Daphne," Marianne chided, as she filled her own plate generously from the offerings of the footman, her thoughts evidently running parallel to Arabella's own. "To say nothing of wrinkles. Fancy having wrinkles before you are twenty, all for the sake of giving the rest of us indigestion by glaring through every meal."

"I'm not trying to give *you* indigestion," Daphne protested pointedly, cutting a glance toward their father. "*You* never tore me away from a holiday I was enjoying, Marianne, nor you either, Arabella."

"And yet, I believe we are the only ones suffering from your punishment, dearest," Marianne pointed out with a glance at Father, who was patently oblivious. "So, you may as well give it up. You can't tell me truthfully that it isn't at least a little bit nice to be home among your own things after nearly two months, can you? The weather is simply gorgeous today, and you can go for a nice long ride this afternoon. There is a lovely breeze rustling the trees."

"It is a howling wilderness here, and I hate it," Daphne returned solemnly. Lord Ashbury set his fork down with a sharp snap, evidently not having been so deaf to the conversation as he had appeared.

"Have you had any interesting correspondence, Father?" Arabella interrupted hastily, before he could begin scolding Daphne. The girl undoubtedly deserved a scolding, but Arabella didn't feel quite up to the task of playing peacekeeper quite so early in the morning. She wanted to nip such encounters in the bud. "Any changes in the neighborhood while we were away, other than the new Dr. Larkin who came in to help Dr. Harding?"

"Humph," breathed her father. "Him." He took a sip of the black tea and grimaced. "I dare say you'll hear all about it when callers begin to trickle in today," Lord Ashbury continued, momentarily distracted at least. "But we evidently have a new neighbor, a Lord Willingham who has inherited the Willowbend Farm. We'll have as little to do with him as possible, the scoundrel."

"Are you acquainted with Lord Willingham, then, Father?" wondered Marianne curiously. It was unlike the earl to interest himself enough in his neighbors to form such firm opinions about their character.

"I've never met the man in my life, thankfully. But he is the heir of John Hayes, old Baron Willingham, who was the most dissolute, depraved wretch to walk this earth."

"I always thought you gave that title to the old Duke of Bramblewood," Arabella said.

"Him too," Father said. "I always considered a small blessing that he didn't bother himself with Willowbend, too small and out of the way to interest a man of his tastes, I suppose."

"Who?" Arabella asked. "The former Duke of Bramblewood or Lord Willingham?"

"Either, I suppose, but I was speaking of Willingham. He does own Willowbend, you know. Of course, the place has been closed for years. If the pup is here, be assured he is up to no good."

"So, you think his heir will have his same unfortunate proclivities as his predecessor?" Marianne tilted her head, as if considering the notion. She was never one to accept general assumptions at face value, and Arabella wondered if she had avoided one family argument only to land directly into another.

"The apple doesn't fall far from the tree," Father muttered.

"That does seem reasonable, if Lord Willingham was raised or influenced by his uncle," Arabella interjected with a pointed stare at Marianne.

"I suppose it does," Marianne relented, taking the hint. To Arabella's satisfaction, she dropped the subject and applied herself to her breakfast.

"Oh, the assumption is quite reasonable, and what's more, it's perfectly obvious," Lord Ashbury retorted testily. "All the money in the world couldn't gild a family that has given itself over to producing such wastrels, no matter how old their title may be. And for that matter, I am given to understand that old Lord Willingham managed to lose practically all the family fortune: quite an accomplishment, actually, as it was really rather vast before he inherited it. I've no doubt whatsoever that his nephew is only darkening our neighborhood because Willowbend farm is very nearly all that remains of his inheritance. As if we wanted some impoverished rake of a fortune hunter in these respectable parts," he muttered.

"Surely, he will remove himself and sell the farm quickly enough, once he sees that no one is going to bother with him," Arabella suggested soothingly, a little alarmed at her father's sudden vehemence. Generally speaking, he did not stir himself to such an extent over the character of their neighbors. Or much else, for that matter. Having been dealt the unbearable blow of losing his beloved wife, Lord Ashbury took refuge in a nearly impenetrable state of indifference. Such fretting was quite unlike him.

"Not If he is as like his uncle as I suspect," her father returned darkly. "There was a man who never cared a whit if his presence was wanted or not if he happened to be determined to inflict himself on some unfortunate soul."

"Why Father, it really sounds as if you knew this late Lord Willingham rather well in your youth," laughed Marianne, heedless of her father's thunderous expression. Really, Arabella thought, sometimes Marianne's quest for knowledge was an anathema. "Was he some manner of rival of yours?" Marianne persisted.

"Hardly," snorted Lord Ashbury contemptuously, but Arabella couldn't help but notice a flicker of some unidentifiable emotion in his steely grey eyes as he spoke, and the teacup rattled as he put it in the saucer with some force. "And this impoverished fool of a nephew of his is hardly worth such a lengthy conversation at my table. Suffice it to say, girls, that we will *not* see the newly titled Lord Willingham in any but the most strictly essential capacity. I have no doubt that such a man would be delighted to ensnare a wealthy, heedless bride, but he will certainly not find it such an easy task with every member of the gentry here turning their backs to him. He will find that Northwickshire is not the backwater he supposes it to be."

"And as he does not sound like the sort of gentleman to enjoy farming, he will doubtless leave as soon as he realizes that," Arabella agreed firmly, seeing that Marianne's curiosity was roused as well as her own.

"Quite so. Now, you will all excuse me, I have a great deal of work to catch up with after such an extended trip," Lord Ashbury said, quite heedless of the fact that his parting remark would rekindle Daphne's nearly forgotten ire. He stood painfully and hobbled from the table, clearly favoring his sore toe.

"Father," began the youngest Sedgewick sister, but Arabella hastily interrupted. "Oh, hush, Daphne," Arabella hissed. She felt almost tempted to give her youngest sister a kick beneath the table, but she could scarcely imagine the uproar that giving in to such an impulse might create. "There simply isn't any *point* in carrying on about it any longer. We are home now."

"If he can get worked up into such a state about the nephew of some dead man he barely knew, he can mind that his own daughter is unhappy," Daphne argued stubbornly. "He *could* care, I just have to find a way to make him. I'll find it one of these days; you mark my words, Arabella Sedgewick. I'll make him notice me."

"Now *there*'s a worrying thought," Marianne murmured, watching Daphne's stormy exit from the breakfast table. "I hate to agree with her when she's in such a state, but really, would it kill Father to give her a bit of notice now and then?"

"I'm sure Father does what he thinks is best," Arabella replied, but she was distracted. It hadn't occurred to her younger sister just then, thankfully, but how many more years might it be, before Daphne realized that creating real scandals and unsuitable connections were far more effective ways to get their father to take notice than damaging property and throwing childish tantrums? Arabella pursed her lips. She should not borrow trouble, she thought.

CHAPTER 3

Later that day, Miss Ellen Millworth came to visit the girls, but Arabella most deliberately. Ellen was a second cousin on Arabella's mother's side, and Mrs. Millworth had been close with Arabella's mother. Although Arabella and Ellen had been friends since infancy, after the death of Lady Ashbury, Arabella became even closer with her cousin, almost as a sister her own age since Ellen was an only child. Mrs. Millworth acted as a surrogate mother in some respects, and the girls had even taken to calling her Aunt Augusta, although her proper title would have been Cousin Augusta. Arabella knew that Ellen would have been waiting with great impatience for it to be late enough in the day for all the proper callers to return to their homes. She was one of the very few people with whom Arabella felt comfortable speaking candidly, and as such, they preferred to exchange their confidences without others present when possible.

Arabella caught her friend's hands in jubilation as Ellen exclaimed. "I am so delighted, selfishly, I admit, that your father decided to cut your holiday short, Arabella." She rapturously embraced her friend and cousin, and looking over her shoulder, she included Marianne in the greeting.

"I cannot claim that I was terribly disappointed myself," admitted Arabella with a warm smile as she rang for a late tea for the three ladies, "although I did feel badly for Daphne. She considered herself quite cheated in the matter."

"Poor Daphne! Where is she?"

"I convinced her to go for a ride," Marianne admitted. "She was not fit for human companionship. I suggested that her mare would not mind her bad temper."

Ellen chuckled. "Ho ho! I am sure she suffered such a grave injustice with quiet dignity and composure," Ellen teased as she settled into her seat.

"Indeed," Marianne said dryly.

Ellen was perhaps the only person outside of the sisters in the Sedgewick family who could tease Arabella about Daphne's escapades, as Arabella knew beyond a shadow of a doubt that Ellen loved Daphne as if she were her own sister.

"Oh certainly, if you consider flinging the luggage into the stables an act of dignity and composure." Arabella shook her head at the memory as she sank into a chair.

"Really, I thought Father was quite brave to make such a decision and court Daphne's wrath so casually."

"But then, *he* was not the one who had to wait until her temper spent itself," Marianne pointed out. "And then, of course, Arabella pointed out what a lot of extra work she had made for the staff by soiling the luggage in such a shocking manner in the first place."

Arabella threw a smile towards the maid who brought in the tea tray with a steaming pot and lemon biscuits. "That's all, Daisy," she said. "I will pour, and we won't be needing anything else."

"Yes, my lady," Daisy said with a curtsey as she left the room.

"Well, if I know Daphne, I am certain she felt terribly remorseful and apologized handsomely," Ellen commented as she took one of her favorite treats and put it on a plate in front of her.

"Yes, *and* she insisted on helping clean up," Marianne added. "I am confident that the neighborhood is still ringing with the scandalous tale of the Earl of Ashbury's youngest daughter scrubbing luggage in the courtyard."

Arabella nodded. "I'm sure several people certainly saw her before we managed to dissuade her from the project."

Ellen chuckled. "Her heart is in the right place."

"Yes," Arabella agreed as she picked up the teapot to pour. "In spite of Daphne's ire, it's very good to be home," she said as she passed a cup to her friend and added cream and sugar to her own tea after pouring Marianne's cup.

"So, you aren't breaking your heart, leaving behind a conquest in Bath?" wondered Ellen archly as she picked up a spoon.

"Oh, dozens, I suppose," Arabella scoffed. "But I'm nowhere close to breaking my heart over any of them. They're no different from the gentlemen one meets in the Ton, after all. I imagine they are all more or less the same, no matter where one goes."

"Perhaps not *all*," Ellen murmured softly, and Arabella was surprised to see a definite blush creeping across her friend's pretty face as she nibbled a biscuit.

"Why, Ellen Millworth!" she exclaimed, setting her teacup down and leaning forward, all exasperation at the insipid quality of eligible bachelors and the constant trial of Daphne's behavior forgotten in an instant. "You meant something very particular by that statement. Don't attempt to deny it. Have you met some gentleman who has inspired your regard?"

"I really and truly have," Ellen admitted, hugging herself and smiling delightedly. "Oh, Arabella, I simply couldn't manage to write about him in any of my letters to you." Ellen included Marianne in her glance, but it was clear she wanted to share the news with Arabella most particularly.

"I tried ever so hard to write a letter, and yet my words all felt short and flat and colorless compared to what I was feeling." She leaned across the table and grasped her friend's hands. "I have just been dying to tell you everything, though."

"Tell me now, and don't leave anything out," ordered Arabella encouragingly as she squeezed Ellen's hand.

Ellen was a very pretty girl, from a genteel and wealthy family, and although her family had no title, Ellen had experienced no shortage of suitors. She had dark and mysterious eyes and a generous head of dark unruly hair, very unlike Arabella's own straight and altogether limp blonde locks. Yet, in spite of her decidedly romantic and dreamy nature, Arabella had never seen her friend look so smitten before. With a quick, envious pang, she wondered what it would be like to have someone inspire such overwhelming emotions. Oh, posh, she thought. She would not feel envious of her dearest friend.

"So, who is he?" Marianne urged, sitting back and nibbling on a biscuit.

"His name is Sir James Randall. He stays primarily in London, but came north briefly on business just a few days after your family left for Bath. He was unable to stay long, unfortunately, but a mere week was practically a lifetime for our hearts, Arabella." She put her teacup aside and dramatically placed her arms across her chest. "I know how foolish that must sound, but I cannot think of any other way of expressing it. We simply fell in love without any regard for the passage of time. I feel as if I have known Sir James a hundred—no, a thousand years at the very least."

"Well, if a thousand years isn't enough time to form a solid opinion of a gentleman's character, then I don't suppose any length of time would suffice," Arabella said lightly. It was jealousy, plain and simple, she told herself sternly, that made her feel so skeptical of her dearest friend's rapturous claim. She worked diligently to keep any doubt out of her expression as she continued to listen to Ellen.

"Exactly so! Besides, we have corresponded steadily all the rest of the summer, and I have always thought it simpler to communicate one's truest feelings and character in a letter than any other medium; don't you think so?"

"Besides being able to tell your closest friend that you are in love, I suppose you mean?"

"Oh, well yes, besides that," laughed Ellen carelessly.

"Do tell," Marianne urged.

Ellen included both young women in her gaze. "I was speaking of becoming acquainted with someone's very *soul*, anyhow, not just telling news. There is such a difference."

"Certainly," Arabella murmured blandly into her tea.

"He is just… splendid. That's really the best word to describe Sir James, I have decided. And I assure you, Arabella, I have given the matter extensive thought! He is positively splendid in every aspect."

"Handsome, I suppose?" prompted Arabella after a moment, as her friend seemed to have become lost in some gauzy daydream about the splendidness of Sir James Randall.

"Terribly handsome, of course," Ellen agreed, smiling infectiously. "*So* dashing and he has the dreamiest gray eyes, with abundant flecks of green; just like the waves of the ocean during a marvelous storm. And the thickest chestnut curls—you know I could never abide the thought of a balding husband, but there seems little chance of that fate for Sir James. And his smile. Oh, he has a smile that makes me simply weak at the knees."

Marianne exchanged a glance with her sister.

"Dear me, he sounds like a rather dangerous creature, my dear." Arabella was a little concerned that her friend was so obviously head over heels for this fellow.

"I suppose he *is* rather dangerous. No man could look so sinfully attractive and be entirely harmless, after all. And he is terribly clever, much more clever than I am. But for all that, he has never even once made me feel like a fool. I shall have to show you his letters." Ellen paused then, looking from Arabella to Marianne, and shook her head. "But no, I couldn't. It would feel almost like betraying a sacred trust. Oh, I hope you aren't hurt by that?" Ellen gnawed worriedly at her bottom lip, gazing beseechingly at Arabella. "I know we have never, ever had secrets from one another, but this-"

"This is different; I quite understand," Arabella said reassuringly, although she was aware of an additional layer of concern having dropped itself most unwelcomely into her mind. "I wouldn't dream of asking to read such private letters—although I have received some quite amusing letters that I will gladly share with *you*, as neither myself nor the authors have even dreamt of being in love with one another, really."

"Oh, I knew you would understand, of course. You always understand, Arabella. Love makes all the difference."

"Of course," Arabella said. "So, you are certain you are in love with Sir James?" Arabella wondered if love would ever hit her with such an irresistible blow. It seemed rather overwhelming and inconvenient. Arabella was not sure she would like to be so out of control of herself as Ellen clearly was. Ellen, however, was always a bit more emotional than Arabella in all things.

"Oh yes!" she gushed. "And I can, of course, *tell* you some of the things Sir James has written to me," Ellen conceded. "You will be able to see just from that how he is such a sensitive, passionate person, and how deeply and unrestrainedly he cares for me."

Arabella pursed her lips, considering. In her mind, love was much more of an action than words on a page. Was that why she was so unmoved by the letters sent to her? Was she an unnatural woman? She wondered, not moved by mere words of love? After all, there were heaps of such words on the pages of letters in her room. None had brought her to Ellen's state of ecstasy.

Ellen's words came back to her then. *Love!* It was indeed dangerous for a young woman to be in love with a man, unless, of course, they had some understanding. Was the man in love with her?

"What of the gentleman's sensibility?" asked Marianne.

"Yes. Ellen, my dear, are you actually engaged to this person?" Arabella asked, throwing caution to the winds at this last statement. "Surely, if he is making such claims of his devotion to you, there is an understanding of some sort between the two of you."

"*Everything* is understood," Ellen said with a blissful sigh, evidently unaware of the sharp tone that had crept into Arabella's voice. "He swore that he was lost, hopelessly lost, the moment he first laid eyes upon me, and has given me a thousand evidences of his continued devotion to me and me alone. Falling in love is just as marvelous as I have always dreamed it might be, Arabella, only infinitely better. But you shall see for yourself in only two days' time!"

"Shall I indeed?"

"Yes, oh I am *so* delighted that your father decided to cut short your stay in Bath, or else you would have missed so much of Sir James' visit. I could not bear it myself. If my parents suggested a trip anywhere just now, I think I would simply die."

"But you aren't going anywhere, so there's no danger of that, thankfully," Arabella couldn't help but laugh good-naturedly at her friend's dreamy distraction. She imagined it was something akin to attempting to have a sensible conversation with an intoxicated person, not that such a thing was within her realm of experiences.

"Of course not, and thank goodness. It would never do to die and miss the rest of my life being in love with Sir James," Ellen agreed seriously. "What a hideous waste *that* would be."

Arabella raised an eyebrow and exchanged glances with Marianne.

"I know you're both laughing at me, and I can hardly blame you. But you must wait until the day after next and you will understand everything perfectly. One has only to gaze upon Sir James to understand how utterly perfect he is."

"I would never dream of laughing at you. Very much," Arabella was compelled by honesty to qualify her protest with a slight smile. "And I am delighted, of course, that you have found such an intoxicating love. I suppose your parents approve of Sir James?"

"In a general sort of sense, yes, they certainly approve of him. Indeed, there is nothing anyone could disapprove of. He is a refined and wealthy gentleman of excellent manners and a flawless reputation. His letters of introduction when he first came into the neighborhood at the beginning of the summer were quite impressive, from what I understood."

"So, he has spoken to your father?"

"He has asked to court you?" Marianne queried.

"Well no."

"He hasn't?" Arabella narrowed her eyes at that.

"Well, I haven't *exactly* told Mama and Papa that Sir James and I have such a strong regard for one another," Ellen said, twisting her napkin in her lap, most unmercifully.

"Why ever not?" demanded Arabella, more surprised by this admission than any other that Ellen had made that afternoon. Mr. and Mrs. Millworth were esteemed and well-to-do members of the gentry, and moreover were both excellent parents, doting on their only child with a warm and attentive affection that had often struck a little pain of jealousy in Arabella's heart when she thought of her own father's indifference. It was unsettling, she thought, to realize just how often she *was* envious of Ellen. She would never before have considered her affection for Ellen to be flawed in even the smallest way.

"Oh, it is hard to say, precisely. I am certain that they *will* approve as soon as Sir James speaks to Papa. Indeed, they will adore him nearly as much as I do!"

"Then why the secrecy?" Marianne asked.

" I have never known either of your parents to deny you any happiness. They will be over-joyed, I am sure," Arabella added.

"Sir James wished to settle some business matters first— the very business matters that have taken him back to Town for so much of the summer, the poor man. I can't imagine a worse place to spend the summer!" She wrinkled her nose at the very thought. "But he felt it best to have everything settled perfectly before speaking to

Papa. He said he didn't want to risk appearing in a less than perfect light, I suppose. He said that he would sooner suffer the agonies of a hundred deaths than risk failing in his pursuit of my hand. And you know, it has been terribly thrilling to have a secret! All of our letters have been passed through the hands of the dear old second gardener at the Rosewood estate."

"Mr. Brum?" Arabella asked, surprised. She exchanged a glance with Marianne.

"The very same."

"You always swore that gardener had the very face of a murderer," Arabella objected, rather foolishly. Somehow Ellen calling the villainous-looking old gardener 'dear' was impossible to ignore. "Why, Ellen, you wouldn't even walk on the same side of the lane as him, your entire life!"

"He isn't so bad after all," Ellen waved a delicate hand dismissively. "Sir James made the arrangement, and although I will admit that I was uncertain at first, I have grown positively fond of the old man. I couldn't mind anyone who brings me that much closer to my beloved, after all."

Arabella looked askance at her friend. "I have to say I do not much like this clandestine affair. Why on earth would the gentleman not tell your parents of his intentions?"

"Oh, he will," Ellen said.

"And even if he did not, what harm could be in correspondence. Your parents would never forbid you. Why should you keep this secret?"

"Only because Sir James asked it of me," Ellen replied in a hard voice, and Arabella realized that she had offended her friend.

"Oh, I am sorry. You know me, Ellen, overly cautious in all regard," she said with a smile. "But it won't be a secret from your parents much longer, will it? The whole affair seems rather scandalous until they are aware and can give their consent."

Ellen softened immediately. "Silly Arabella, always so worried about being associated with even the tiniest of scandals," laughed Ellen, and Arabella's feelings were thoroughly stung although she was glad a smile tugged at Ellen's lips. Ellen, out of everyone in the entire world outside of the Sedgewick family, knew perfectly well Arabella's reasons for wanting to stay well away from even a whisper of scandal.

"Arabella is only concerned for your own sake, Ellen," Marianne said as Arabella drew back from her friend.

"Such a thing could ruin a young lady, after all."

"I'm so sorry, I spoke very carelessly," Ellen was instantly contrite, her large brown eyes filling with understanding tears. "I wasn't thinking at all, you know that's always the trouble with me. I get caught up with something and become terribly heedless about everything else. I hope you can forgive me; I really am ever so sorry I snapped at you."

"Of course, I forgive you, you goose," Arabella said, thawing as she always did. There had never been even a whisper of malice in Ellen's character, and she knew it well. "Consider it forgotten."

"Well, *I* shall not forget it. As wonderful as being in love is, I would hate to think that it makes me become an inconsiderate friend. And you must put your mind at rest, at any rate, for Sir James plans to speak to Papa this very week and everything will be all out in the open and as respectable as anyone could wish."

"That does make me feel better, I suppose. And I'm really terribly happy for you, I hope I don't seem otherwise. It's only just so sudden for me, I mean. So, I must take a little bit of time to get used to the idea of my best friend being in love."

"I still feel as if I needed some time to get used to the idea myself," Ellen confessed, her smile turning shy suddenly. "It is wonderful, of course, but I do have the oddest feeling now and then that everything is changing so quickly, I can scarcely keep my head."

"We knew it would all change, when we came out," Arabella reminded her friend. "I hope this Sir James doesn't intend to take you very far away? I could scarcely forgive him or any other man a crime as terrible as *that*."

"Certainly not, we shall stay close by. At least, I suppose we shall," Ellen trailed off, looking uncertain. "I don't actually know that we've discussed such a thing, come to think of it, but he did have business here as well as in London. Oh dear, do you suppose he shall want to live in London?"

"You hardly could until things are more ...conventionally understood between you two. But he simply must be brought around to the idea of staying near here, you know, at least for the summers. I have decided that proximity is just about the most important factor I can have in settling on my own match."

"You don't really mean that," laughed Ellen. "You couldn't really marry someone you weren't in love with simply because they lived nearby."

"I don't see an alternative. No one I have ever met has caused me even a thousandth of the feeling that you have for your Sir James, you know. But the thing must be done, and I really do have to marry someone who is *fairly* close by, or else I fear Daphne will run absolutely wild."

"Yes," Marianne laughed. "I have no intention of taking her in hand. That is all on you, Arabella."

"But you've taken our neighborhood's only eligible visitor, though, so I don't know who that leaves me with," Arabella laughed as she spoke, but a hint of bitterness must have slipped past her careful guard, because Ellen gave her hand an affectionate and understanding squeeze.

"There is that new owner of Willowbend farm, Lord Willingham. He is terribly handsome," she suggested helpfully. "Indeed, I don't know that I wouldn't have set my cap for him if I hadn't already fallen just fathoms deep in love with Sir James. Lord Willingham is younger than I expected, and has a fierce sort of manner and shadowy reputation that is rather fascinating. But why are you laughing, Arabella? Marianne?"

"Father was just telling us this morning that we are in no way to acknowledge Lord Willingham," Marianne said.

"Yes. Evidently is bound to be a great rogue like his uncle before him. And I don't think a single one of my callers today has failed to mention what a suspicious character he is, for that matter. He hardly seems a likely prospect for me," Arabella giggled at the very idea. It was not just Ellen who knew of Arabella's mania for remaining vigilantly proper and perfectly decorous. She had gained something of a reputation in the Ton for having nothing to do with any gentleman who had the slightest blemish in his history.

"Oh, very well, I suppose he wouldn't do at all for you," Ellen admitted a little reluctantly. "But his shadowy reputation does seem a bit romantic, *I* think. And there is something about his eyes that makes me think he can't be entirely a rogue. In fact, he seems…" she paused searching for a word. "Wholesome," she said.

Arabella laughed outright. "The whole of the town has branded him a rogue and you call him wholesome! No doubt your vision is colored a bit by love, I should say," Arabella rejoined lightly, smiling affectionately at her friend. "But it hardly makes a difference to me if the man is entirely a rogue or only one tenth a rogue. I have very painstakingly narrowed down my list of suitors to three upstanding and suitable gentlemen, and Lord Willingham is most definitely not one of them."

CHAPTER 4

Christopher Hayes, Baron Willingham, wanted to get an early start. He surveyed the dilapidated and unpromising- looking stables that graced his farm, feeling a surge of determination that almost surprised him. It was foolishly optimistic, he knew, to look at the sad near- ruin and feel anything but discouraged, but he couldn't help but see the potential in the building, and more, in the entire property. Willowbend Farm was small, hopelessly old-fashioned, and pitifully neglected, and yet he had felt a connection with it from the moment he set foot on its sodden, weedy ground. The fact that it grew weeds, gave proof that the soil was not entirely devoid of nutrients for crops, unlike the rocky soil of the barony. Now, in the early morning light, the farm seemed quaint, if not impressive.

He hadn't expected that instant, undeniable feeling in his blood at taking ownership of a farm he had never seen before in his life. Truly, Christopher couldn't say precisely what he *had* expected when he made the journey to the only bit of his inheritance that remained. The fact that his uncle hadn't considered Willowbend Farm worth selling or gambling away hadn't been particularly encouraging, as his uncle had pawned or lost practically everything else of value belonging to the Willingham estate.

Shaking his head a little at the memory, Christopher made his way gingerly through the entrance of the stables. He had been inside a few times previously, investigating just how much damage there was to the deserted structure. Work was scheduled to begin on repairs, although none of his ragged band of laborers had bothered to make their entrance. They were as dubious about the restoration project as Christopher knew he ought to be, and yet, he couldn't claim to be offering the highest wages. Anytime a better- paying workday presented itself he was left quite unapologetically behind, which made progress frustratingly slow.

At least he wouldn't have to waste any more of his time and sadly limited resources on repairing the house itself. The manor house of Willowbend Farm was undoubtedly lovely at one point in the dim past, but it had been abandoned and barely habitable for years.

The roof leaked into the upstairs bedrooms and ran through the walls into the dining room. Mold grew on the wallpaper in the drawing room and in what he had assumed was once the music room. The entire place had a musty smell that made Christopher sneeze. He was sure that it was not good for his constitution, and so he had ordered the entire section of the house torn down, saving the stones from the hearth and fire place in each room. He approved the remainder of the house, including the stone enforced kitchen and the servant's wing above it, although both needed a thorough cleaning.

Christopher had begrudgingly ordered a minimum of repairs so that a housekeeper and small staff would agree to stay, but homemaking was hardly a priority for a lone man with a fortune to earn. His own room, which once belonged to the butler, was above the kitchen. It was a warm and charming room, especially considering the state of the rest of the house. He knew most people would fix the house before the stable, but if he was to grow his fortune, he must first take care of the horses which he hoped would be his salvation. Hopefully, with the good land in the area, and some luck with the horses, he may even be able to buy back the lost lands surrounding the barony.

Surprisingly, while growing up with his wastrel uncle, he had forgone the man's tutelage in gambling and instead concentrated on the horses themselves. He knew how to pick good bloodlines. Now, he only had to afford a reputable stallion and a couple of hardy mares to begin to bring back his fortune. The stable first, and then the house, he told himself.

Besides, he reflected ruefully, picking up stray rotten planks as he walked through the stables, it wasn't as though he would be entertaining any time soon. His uncle's scandalous reputation had certainly cut out that expense for him, for hardly a soul in the village or any of the neighboring estates had a civil word for him.

Resigning himself to another day's lost labor due to his missing workmen, Christopher stripped off his linen jacket and rolled up his sleeves. The fortunate thing about inheriting such a shocking reputation he thought philosophically, as he began to work in earnest, was that it hardly mattered if he shocked the village further by engaging in common physical labor.

※

ARABELLA URGED HER MOUNT ONWARD, HER EYES scanning the foggy morning distance as she searched for Daphne. Drat the girl, she thought, momentarily giving in to the urge to scowl since there was no one around to see her, anyway. It was positively ungrateful of Daphne to take advantage of her offer of an early morning ride by promptly galloping away. For all it was late summer, the weather was unseasonably damp and chilly with a feel of the coming autumn in the air, and Arabella had been regretting her magnanimous suggestion even before Daphne had disappeared into the mists. The odds were slim that Daphne would get lost or injured, but Arabella knew she wouldn't be able to rest easily until she had the wretched child in her sight once more.

Arabella was a decently accomplished horsewoman, and actually harbored a secret love of riding, but had always made a point of only riding as much as was strictly ladylike. Considering Daphne's unpredictable impulses, it really would have been an advantage, she reflected in irritated hindsight, to have indulged herself a little more. It had most likely been only a matter of time before she would have ended up riding about in the fog searching for her sister.

"Daphne! Daphne Sedgewick!" she called, throwing decorum and caution both to the wind for once. She couldn't help but picture the child thrown from her mount, lost and cold and in pain somewhere in the rather wild fields that bordered their family's estate. There *was* the pond at the bend in the road, she remembered, her blood promptly turning to ice in her veins at the thought. It was terribly deep, and with a steep drop-off that had always discouraged wading of any sort. If the mist was dense enough, and Daphne had galloped recklessly enough, she might have plunged in over her depth before she even saw the water. Daphne couldn't swim, of course, not that any woman could hope to swim when her skirts would weigh her down, and who knew what her horse might do in such a situation. She would drown, just as their mother had, all because Arabella had wanted to distract her from her ill-temper.

Heart racing, Arabella pushed her own mount to a reckless pace, to find her younger sister, panic leaving very little room in her mind for anything else. The surrounding fields and woods couldn't possibly have been very far from the Sedgewick estate, but between the heavy morning mist and her own frantic anxiety the landscape seemed utterly foreign. With nothing else to guide her search, Arabella turned toward a faint but persistent sound of hammering, thinking that perhaps whoever was causing the racket had seen Daphne ride past and could give her some idea of the direction.

As she drew nearer to the sound it was joined by a murmur of voices, and suddenly Daphne's unmistakable bell-like laugh rang out quite clearly. Arabella's fear evaporated instantly at the sound, to be replaced by a rush of annoyance at Daphne's thoughtlessness and her own foolish panic. Arabella slowed her rather bewildered mount to a more decorous pace and attempted to compose her expression as she approached the sadly dilapidated stable that emerged from the mist.

"Oh, *there* you are Arabella, I thought you were right behind me and then the next thing I knew, you had just disappeared," Daphne called out, carelessly cheerful.

"It is you who disappeared," Arabella muttered. She noted that Daphne had dismounted her mare and was standing beside it, conversing animatedly with a handsome, hatless laborer who had his shirtsleeves rolled up past his elbows.

Drawing her eyes from the man's impressive biceps, Arabella felt a renewed sense of annoyance. "That's hardly surprising, considering the way you raced off without a warning," Arabella returned as evenly as she could manage. "I was worried that you had gotten lost in all of this fog."

"I didn't get lost. Exactly," Daphne hedged, exchanging a conspiratorial glance with the laborer. "I just wasn't entirely sure where I *was*. So, I stopped to ask for directions, and then I got terribly interested in the work. Did you know, Arabella, he is going to restore this old stable? I would have thought it was a hopeless ruin, but apparently there is life in it yet."

Arabella's eyes were drawn to the previously mentioned dilapidated stable and then unerringly back to the handsome laborer, who stood with a smile on his face as he looked down at her irascible sister. He had remarkably even white teeth, Arabella thought. For a laborer. And stormy gray eyes. No, she corrected herself they were blue, a dark midnight blue. What was she about, noticing a laborer's eyes? It was borderline indecent. Her eyes strayed again to his impressive forearms which were tanned by the sun. Yes, well, noticing his biceps or his forearms, was not particularly decent either. She brought herself firmly back to the present.

"Isn't that a wonderful thought?" continued Daphne. "I love the idea of something looking hopeless but really still having hope."

"Yes, it's very admirable, I am sure," Arabella said firmly. She knew that Daphne was perfectly capable of rhapsodizing over the old barn or whatever it was for a quarter of an hour at least, with no thought for the work she was apparently interrupting or the sister who was ready to box her ears. "And I am very grateful to you, sir, for giving my little sister assistance and allowing her to disrupt your labor. We will not take up any more of your time."

※

"I don't mind the interruption; I can assure you," Christopher replied gravely, as he pulled down the sleeves of his shirt, a little tardily, he imagined. He gave a little nod of his head. The stiff, although decidedly beautiful, lady had evidently mistaken him for a farm laborer, and he saw no reason to correct her. She had looked horrified enough at the sight of her sister conversing with a working man. He could only imagine her dismay at finding out that their new acquaintance was the wicked Lord Willingham instead. "I can't think of the last time I had such an interesting conversation. May I be so bold as to offer my assistance in regaining your seat, Miss Sedgewick?"

"Oh certainly, thank you. Arabella would most likely die of horror if I were to climb back up by myself," Daphne answered merrily, taking Christopher's hand as if they were friends of long acquaintance.

"We wouldn't want that, now, would we?" he chuckled as he expertly helped her into the side saddle.

Perhaps he was not a laborer, but a groom, Arabella considered. After all, he was working on the stable. It did not matter. Both were well below hers or Daphne's notice. It did not matter how extraordinarily arresting the man was, with his broad toothy smile, and steely blue eyes. His skin had an indecorous tan from working out of doors, and his hair, she noted, was bleached by the sun to a pale blonde, but she could note a tinge of ginger. She blinked and looked away. A lady did not give such men a second look. Honestly, Daphne had no sense of decorum.

Arabella did her best to pretend she hadn't heard the exchange between the man and her sister, writhing internally at Daphne's shocking disregard for propriety. When she got her alone, she just might box the little minx's ears.

"There you are now," the man said as he settled Daphne on her mount. "I note that the fog is lifting nicely. It'll be just a five minutes ride west across that field and you will find yourselves at the main lane. Another few minutes along that lane and you will find yourselves on the North Road."

"Thanks ever so much, and good luck with your stables," Daphne called, already urging her mare forward. Arabella checked her impulse to call Daphne back, knowing it would do little good once the girl had decided to move. It would be unendurable to lose her sister twice in one morning, so Arabella only shook her head.

"Thank you again for your assistance," Arabella said distractedly, sparing not another glance at the roughly attractive man.

"Not at all," he answered politely enough, and she wondered why she had the feeling that he was laughing at her somehow. His stormy grey eyes were sparkling.

No, they were blue. Surely, they were midnight blue. It hardly mattered, of course, and she set her horse across the field before she lost sight of Daphne entirely.

She put the man entirely out of her mind. Almost entirely. Why, she wondered, were the most extraordinarily good-looking gentlemen so unreachable.

CHAPTER 5

Arabella found herself out of patience with her younger sister. "Really, you don't deserve to come to the party with us Daphne, not when I can't trust you to behave yourself for even five minutes at a time," Arabella snapped the words out with more vehemence than either of her sisters were accustomed to hearing from her. They both gazed at her with frank surprise as she snatched up Daphne's newest gown and whirled it about, ostensibly for an inspection. It was blue and silver silk with a single line of embroidery of leaves on the train. It was simple for a girl who was not yet out, but lovely nonetheless.

"Are you feeling quite yourself, Arabella?" Daphne found her voice first and spoke much more meekly than *she* was accustomed to do. "Are you well?"

"Certainly, I am well; why would you ask that?"

"Only, you seem frightfully cross just now, and I can't remember a time when you *ever* seemed so cross," Daphne answered earnestly. "Not even lots of times when I've been much worse behaved than this morning."

"Perhaps I ought to have gotten cross with you all of those times too, and then you might have learned not to act like such a perfect heathen," Arabella retorted. She stared at the gown in her hands, vaguely angry that she could find no fault with it. "Isn't that what you're always telling me, Marianne?"

"Yes, more or less, I suppose," Marianne nodded slowly and took the gown gently out of her older sister's hands. "But I don't believe I meant for you to scold Daphne for a decade's worth of naughtiness all at once, dearest."

"Better late than never," Arabella snapped. "The idea of stopping for a friendly chat with a strange working man, to say nothing of scaring me half to death in the first place by racing away in such a manner!"

Daphne opened her mouth to retort, but Arabella stopped her with a finger before her nose. "You knew full well that you had left me behind, so do not say anything to the contrary. Why Daphne Sedgewick, I would have thought you'd have more sense than to initiate a conversation with a strange man. You are fourteen-years-old! Girls your age have been ruined by far less, you know."

"There, now, she isn't ruined," Marianne said reassuringly. "It isn't so terribly improper to ask for directions, after all."

"You know what I mean, Marianne. She isn't a child, really, any longer, and we must all realize that her foolish escapades can have very real, lasting consequences," snapped Arabella.

"I *won't* be talked about as if I wasn't even in the room," Daphne interjected, temper ominously building in her expression. "Or as if I were some horrid problem that needed to be solved instead of a live, breathing person."

"Oh, child, that isn't what she meant," Marianne said.

"Daphne," Arabella began. Too late, Arabella realized the damage she had caused. She could see the anger boiling in her sister's eyes.

"It *is* what she meant! I'm not a fool, Arabella," Daphne shouted. "And I'm not a child, Marianne."

"A lady does not shout," Arabella began, trying reasonably to calm the situation, but the words just seemed to inflame Daphne. "Well, I shan't shout at your precious soiree," Daphne shouted. "In fact, you needn't worry about my behaving badly at the party. I won't be going at all."

"Now, Daphne, don't be silly," Arabella tried to soothe her, reaching out but Daphne shrugged her off, screaming defiantly at her older sister. "No! Silly Daphne! Problem Daphne. You can go without me and have a lovely time, and not concern yourself at all with my being a heathen or silly or anything. You are better off without me!"

Arabella tried a different tack. "Daphne, don't be ridiculous," she said with some sternness. "The Millworths are expecting us. It is highly rude to ignore an invitation after it has been accepted. Now, get dressed."

"No! I said I'm not going!" Daphne, in a fit of pique, suddenly seized the gown from Marianne and settled the matter by flinging the expensive garment into the fireplace, which unfortunately was blazing merrily just then. The fine silk instantly caught and shriveled, a bead of black ash against silver, melting to nothingness.

The maid let out a distressed gasp and rushed to attempt to rescue the costly garment. She managed to drag it from the flames before the silver thread was entirely consumed, but it was irrevocably ruined. Daphne stormed out of the room, and Arabella sat down helplessly.

"There now, Letty, there's no sense scorching yourself," Marianne said as Letty tried to stop the gown from burning by beating it with her apron. "The poor gown is ruined beyond all repair," Marianne said, seeing that Arabella was in no state to take charge of matters. "We will find what is left of the silver thread when the ash has cooled."

"It was the loveliest gown, and looked so perfect on Miss Daphne," the maid mourned, watching pieces of the silken ribbons turn to black ash. "It'll take at least a fortnight to have another one so nice made up, and you know she hasn't anything else decent to wear tonight, not since she gave away so many of her dresses last week."

"I'm sure Miss Daphne was perfectly in earnest when she said she had no intention of going to the soiree tonight, Letty, so we needn't bother about finding something for her to wear," soothed Marianne, not even bothering to sigh.

Arabella, as the eldest, was generally the one who dealt with managing the staff, but she just didn't have the energy for it. She watched Marianne do her best to calm the distressed maid. "Why don't you go on down and have a nice cup of tea, Letty, and we'll just send for the dressmaker tomorrow?"

"Thank you, Miss," sniffled Letty, preparing to exit the room with all possible haste, but still shooting a concerned backwards glance at Arabella who had not moved from her spot. "Shall I have some tea sent up here as well?" Letty asked.

"I think that would be an excellent idea," Marianne said, after waiting a moment and seeing that Arabella had evidently not heard the question.

"Well, that was unexpected, I must say," she said, sitting next to Arabella once the door had closed behind Letty.

"Not really," Arabella said. "You know Daphne is willful."

"But ordinarily you are the person putting out Daphne's little fires, not deliberately fanning them. And that is very nearly not a figure of speech in this particular case."

"I can't imagine what came over me," Arabella managed, barely, to speak without bursting into tears as she gazed transfixed as the flames danced in the fireplace.

"She *was* quite naughty, but no more than one generally expects from Daphne. I wonder why it annoyed you so particularly this time."

"Annoyed is a very gracious way of putting it, Marianne. The truth is that I simply lost my temper, and my head along with it. I was frightened today, first by the thought that she might have gotten lost and hurt herself, and then by the sight of her speaking so familiarly with that worker. *We* all think of her as a spoiled, headstrong child, and I have no doubt that she thinks of herself that way as well. But it struck me, quite terribly, that Society will very shortly stop seeing her in that light. She is a young lady, and Society will be brutal to her if she persists, to say nothing of a husband. The idea fairly took my breath away with fear for her."

"Daphne wouldn't ever do anything truly wicked, you know," said Marianne soothingly. "At heart, I often think she is the best of us."

"Best?" Arabella said askance. "If she threw an expensive garment like that into the fire, a husband is like to beat her. Truthfully, if Father knew, even he would be angry."

"If he noticed at all," Marianne added.

"Is that the problem, do you think?"

"Perhaps."

Arabella sighed. "It's just sometimes a bit hard to see the goodness beneath all of her wildness."

"Of course, I know that," Marianne added.

"What's mortifying to realize is that I didn't lose my temper just now because I was vexed at Daphne. I lost it because I'm furious with myself for failing her," Arabella said flatly. She could be composed and calm once more, which was a small relief.

"Why, Arabella Sedgewick, what nonsense are you saying? You haven't failed her!"

"I have, though," Arabella turned her gaze from the fireplace to meet her sister's eyes levelly. "I've spent years doing absolutely everything I could to keep the peace in this family; to keep Father from having to be distressed or annoyed by anything, and to keep Daphne happy at all costs. And do you know, I think I have actually made everything worse through all of my efforts. Father has forgotten that he ought to trouble himself about us at all, and Daphne has grown up without the slightest idea that there might be real consequences for her impulsive and foolish choices."

"You've left two members of the family out of your little list, dearest," Marianne said gently. "You have taken great pains to ensure that practically none of the bother of running a household fell to me, didn't you?"

"Well, you hate all of that sort of thing," Arabella said, a little confusedly. Whatever she had expected Marianne's response to be, that was hardly it. "Approving menus, arranging flowers, dealing with servants and seating charts and all."

"Do *you* enjoy it?" demanded Marianne ruthlessly.

"Oh, well no, but I don't mind it either. And I certainly wouldn't care to be shut up in the library for hours on end, studying goodness knows what in some hideously difficult language, which seems to give you such enjoyment."

"And I have the luxury of enjoying my studies because you *do* take on all the household things. I don't really think you've failed Daphne or Father or myself either, although it wouldn't hurt any of us a bit to deal with the unpleasant things that you shield us from all the time. But what of yourself, Arabella? Here you are planning to choose a husband with a great deal less enthusiasm than you might have in choosing a new hat, because you think it's what is expected of you."

"This isn't about that," Arabella interrupted hotly, annoyed at Marianne for bringing the conversation around to a topic she did not wish to discuss.

"What is it about?" Marianne asked, and Arabella had to consider. She supposed, seeing Daphne speaking to the half-dressed laborer, flirting in fact, brought to mind how easily her younger sister could be ruined. Was that truly the reason, she wondered, or was it because she thought the laborer was handsome, and it was clear he could not be a suitor. How could all of her suitors leave her cold, and this man…this laborer, stir her blood. Her feelings seemed to be a maelstrom of conflicting emotions, and she had no idea how to calm the storm inside of herself. She always knew how to calm the storms. Why was this so different?

"I suppose, I am angry with myself for not having properly prepared Daphne for adulthood," she said carefully. "And I am more than a little worried at the prospect of having to correct my error in judgment at such a late point. That is *all*."

But of course, that was not all her heart protested. Combined into the mix was a very real sense of desire for a common laborer. That would not do at all. He absolutely would not fit into Arabella Sedgewick's very ordered life. She sought the cool reserve she had so cultivated since Mother's death. Breathe in. Breathe out, she commanded herself. This would not ruffle her.

"Very well, then, I won't press the matter any further, only I will say that Mother would never have wanted you to sacrifice so much of your own happiness just to keep the rest of the world from experiencing a bit of discomfort. You had better finish getting ready to go to the Millworth's party now. Ellen would be devastated if you don't go."

"What about you?" asked Arabella.

"I'll stay home with Daphne and do my best to keep her from destroying anything else of particular value. No, don't bother arguing with me," Marianne said quickly, seeing that her sister was on the point of protesting. "If you stay, in your current frame of mind, you will doubtless get into another fight with her. Heaven knows I have no real desire to spend my evening dancing with our leaden-footed neighbors and exchanging vapid pleasantries, anyway. You, at least, will have Ellen to distract you. Come home in a better humor."

Arabella half rose from her seat before changing her mind and letting Marianne briskly exit without another word. She felt certain that she *would* burst into tears if she said anything just then, and anyhow, Marianne was perfectly correct in her assessment of the situation.

Perhaps in her assessment of everything, Arabella considered reluctantly, Marianne was right, and that was an unwelcome thought. In all of her efforts to be proper and controlled, had she somehow turned herself into someone incapable of falling in love, and done herself just as large a disservice as she had evidently done to Daphne? Judging from her dizzying conversation with Ellen, falling in love seemed like an act that required at least a fair amount of recklessness, and recklessness was something, in which, she had never been willing to indulge.

At least, not since the day of her mother's death. She had been twelve, a child herself, but forced to grow up so quickly. Arabella thought she might live to be one hundred and she would still be able to hear her father's heartbroken, impassioned sobs as he railed against the reckless, impulsive actions which had brought his beloved to such a senseless and untimely fate. She could hear them ringing in her ears with perfect, tortuous clarity, even though he had hidden in his library to sob. Arabella had to take a deep breath to steady herself enough to block out the memory of her stalwart father so bereft. Men, especially fathers were supposed to be pillars of strength. She could remember how his tears had shaken her, and she endeavored to protect her sisters from realizing how precarious their father's strength really was.

She wondered now, how had it never occurred to her, in all her years of making sure she never behaved impulsively and never caused her father to revisit such anguish, that although she herself was almost preternaturally calm and deliberate in every action, she allowed Daphne to be as reckless as her childish heart could desire?

Arabella knew the answer, of course. She had only thought to keep poor little Daphne happy, to make her feel so loved and doted upon that she might not miss the mother that she had barely known. It had been foolishly short-sighted, but then, Arabella had been a grieving child herself at the time and it had somehow never occurred to her to reevaluate things as they grew older. It had simply become the way they all lived, not something that needed to be questioned or considered.

The time for questioning had come, she supposed, sighing wearily and blinking away tears. But any more introspection could fortunately be put off for the moment at least because she really did have to dress for the evening. She could easily make excuses for Daphne and Marianne's absence, but it would hardly do for all of them to miss the Millworth's party.

PART II

CHAPTER 6

Arabella arrived late to the Millworth soirée, but she knew, Ellen Millworth, her cousin would not much mind. Ellen, just a few months her junior, had always been her best friend. Arabella was looking forward to seeing her after their holiday in Bath.

"Arabella! Over here!" Ellen's enthusiastic greeting was a welcome distraction from the dismal thoughts that kept persistently nagging at Arabella's mind all evening. Several of her acquaintances had actually asked her if she was feeling well, a thing which Arabella could not recall ever happening in the past. It had always been virtually effortless for her to keep a serene, polite expression fixed on her face no matter how much internal strife she might be feeling, but evidently that particular talent had deserted her.

"Why, you are looking quite well-pleased with yourself," she said, crossing to Ellen, who was all but glowing with happiness. "I believe you must have had a much nicer sort of day than I."

"Haven't you had a good day, darling? I can't imagine that is possible, for this is certainly the most wonderful, glorious day in the entire history of days! Stand a little closer to me and you won't be able to help but catch some of my happiness. You do know that joy is contagious."

"That is true all the time. You are just one of those fortunate people who seem to radiate gladness," Arabella said with a laugh, her smile feeling genuine for the first time all evening. "But why is today so particularly wonderful and glorious?"

"You will see and hear for yourself very shortly, but I cannot possibly wait any longer to tell you," Ellen bubbled, her eyes dancing. "You know I had said that Sir James would be returning, and that he would speak to Papa?"

"Of course. I take it he has made it here according to plan, then?"

"He arrived just this morning. Well, it was nearly noon, and I was fraught with worry, but that doesn't really matter now since he is here. I'm so happy and excited I can barely think straight!"

"You must make an effort, dearest, or else I may die of the suspense," Arabella prompted. "Who is this man who has so obviously captured your heart."

"Sir James Randall," she gushed with a hand over her heart.

Arabella chuckled. "Sir James arrived, suffice it to say..."

"Yes, exactly! And he had evidently come directly to call on us, not even stopping at his lodgings first. Mama and Papa were rather amazed, of course, for as far as they knew, he was merely an acquaintance. But he explained everything so beautifully, and so eloquently, and made Papa see that he was truly, ardently in love with me. Oh, it was just like a wonderful dream!"

"And your parents were not cross at all to find out that you had been secretly corresponding with this Sir James nearly all summer long?" wondered Arabella, casting her glance about the crowded room for Mr. and Mrs. Millworth. She had always known them to be doting parents, but that seemed to be taking things rather far, all the same.

"Oh, well, Sir James didn't explain *exactly* that. I daresay he is far too honorable to say anything that might cast a negative light on me, you know," Ellen admitted, a little sheepishly as she took a glass of punch from the tray a footman offered.

"You mean he lied to them?" Arabella asked, coming back to the conversation.

"Certainly not!" Ellen said sharply, quite unlike herself. Arabella seemed to be inciting indignation in everyone today, she thought. She bit her lip and then took a small sip of the drink in her hand.

"He didn't say one word that wasn't strictly true," Ellen continued. "He explained how he had fallen madly in love with me when we met. And how he had rushed back to London to get all of his business affairs perfectly in order so that he might make the best possible impression when he spoke to Papa. He explained that it had taken so long that he was nearly frantic with impatience, and could scarcely bear another second without reaching an understanding."

Judging from Ellen's expression, Arabella thought it was evident that her friend considered the explanation to be perfectly truthful and logical. It was on the tip of her tongue to point out, as gently as she could, that such gaping omissions were tantamount to outright falsehoods, when Ellen gave a barely muffled squeal of delight and crushed Arabella's hand.

"There he is, Arabella, just coming in and waiting to be announced," Ellen gasped breathlessly, all of her attention riveted on the entryway. "Oh, isn't he marvelous?"

Arabella turned to gaze upon this Adonis as her friend spoke. "I dare say, I'm sure he is, but it's terribly difficult to see through the tears in my eyes just now. You've all but broken my hand you know," answered Arabella, tugging her hand out of Ellen's vice-like grasp and smoothing her gloves with over- exaggerated fussiness.

"Oh, I'm sorry!" Ellen's remorse flared quickly, but she was distracted almost immediately by the announcement of one Sir James Randall. Her dearest friend was immediately forgotten. Arabella could not be miffed at the exclusion. After all, Ellen was in love. Arabella was entirely prepared to love the man too, as Ellen's dearest friend.

Sir James was almost as handsome as Ellen had claimed, although not quite as handsome as the unknown laborer, she met today, Arabella thought. She shook off the unwelcome notion that had popped unbidden into her mind. Instead, she gave her attention to her friend's fiancé. He was tall and dashing. He walked through the room with a careless grace that drew a great many eyes, not just Ellen's and Arabella's. Something about his manner and bearing seemed to make every other gentleman in the room look stiff and awkward by comparison. His green eyes and dark gold hair might not have inspired Arabella to the dizzying poetic heights that Ellen had entertained, but she had to admit that he was attractive. When he caught sight of Ellen through the crowd and aimed a devastating smile at her, however, Arabella saw that her friend had not been exaggerating when she had described its potency.

"Oh!" Ellen cried clinging to Arabella's arm as she gazed at her love.

"Good heavens, Ellen, you can't *actually* go weak at the knees every time the man smiles at you," Arabella murmured, torn between the desire to laugh at her friend and the desire to shake some sense into her, but then, Arabella had always been eminently practical. She had to be since her mother had passed.

"I suppose I shouldn't, it's dreadfully inconvenient, but it's simply delicious at the same time," breathed Ellen as Sir James approached them.

"Miss Millworth, I pray that I find you well this evening," Sir James said, the formality of his bow to both ladies in direct contrast with the banked passion that seemed to burn in his eyes.

"You find me a great deal better than well," Ellen answered, barely remembering to curtsey in response, or to breathe, from what Arabella could tell. "As you must surely know."

Arabella supposed that she couldn't really blame Sir James for looking so besotted as he gazed down at Ellen. Excitement and happiness had lent a glow of beauty to her friend that was all but blinding. She did resent, however, that the man did not entirely lose his expression of frank admiration when he turned his eyes toward herself. If he were really so in love with Ellen, he had no business eyeing anyone else with that knowing, appreciative smolder. It made Arabella uncomfortable.

"Oh, my manners and my memory both are shockingly bad this evening, I do apologize," Ellen said, after a brief pause. "Sir Randall, may I introduce my dearest friend in all the world, Lady Arabella Sedgewick."

"Lady Arabella Sedgewick," he repeated. There was *something* that flickered just for an instant in Sir James' eyes as he exchanged a formal greeting with Arabella, she was positive. Her discomfort with the man was increasing with every second that she remained in his presence, but she forced herself to keep her expression carefully neutral as Ellen continued to chatter blithely on.

"Arabella and her family have only just returned from Bath a few short days ago, that is why you did not meet them at your earlier visit, you know, Sir James. But I believe I have mentioned her quite often in my letters-"

"Miss Millworth," Sir James murmured, managing to make the two words both a warning and an endearment, and raising his eyebrows meaningfully.

"What? Oh, no, there is no need to feel alarmed," Ellen laughed, but lowered her voice obligingly. "I have taken Arabella into my confidences, and you may be assured that she is the very soul of discretion. Why, I am utterly certain that she has said nothing even to her younger sister, Miss Marianne Sedgewick. Where is Marianne, Arabella? I haven't seen her here this evening, but I cannot claim to have been paying very close attention to anything aside from my own perfect happiness." Ellen glanced about the room belatedly realizing that she should have inquired earlier.

"Marianne stayed home with Daphne," Arabella said, feeling it best to leave the matter at that. Ellen would understand the implication, that Daphne had been particularly trying, and although she might be privy to Sir James' private affairs, Arabella had no intention of divulging her own to him. "And you may certainly put your mind at ease on my account, Sir James. If Ellen's parents are satisfied with your explanation, then I can certainly have nothing to say on the matter."

"Ah, and you have very diplomatically avoided saying the thing outright, but I believe that I am correct in thinking that you do not entirely approve of the secrecy surrounding our love?" Sir James asked shrewdly, and again Arabella thought she saw something unpleasant cross his gilded, handsome countenance for just an instant.

"It is rather odd, but my approval can be of no consequence," she pointed out calmly. "As I hold no authority over my friend. Undoubtedly you are aware already that a secret correspondence carried with it the risk of exposing both yourself and Miss Millworth to public censure, but I believe a great many people have found such risks in the name of love to be both noble and correct."

"A great many people, but you do not include yourself among them, do you? I suspect a suitor would be quite hard-pressed to inspire you to risk public censure, Lady Arabella."

"I cannot imagine why any suitor of mine should wish to inspire such a thing," returned Arabella. "But my opinion on the matter really has no bearing, as it is already done with, for one thing. And I am certain that you will assure me that you will do everything within your power to make my friend perfectly happy for the rest of her days."

"I shall indeed assure you of that, Lady Arabella, but I am not certain that you will easily take me on my word for it," Sir James said, and Arabella felt confident that his lightly mocking tone was deliberately intended to make her seem foolish.

"I am delighted to take you on your word, Sir Randall," she countered, "I assume it is a worthy word." Yet again she saw that indefinable flicker in Sir James' green eyes. Perhaps he had caught her subtle insinuation, although it had sailed happily over Ellen's head, that his word had not been without shortcomings thus far.

"How fortunate for me. And how wonderful for Miss Millworth, that she has such a fierce and devoted friend as yourself. Of course, I am quite unsurprised to find that such a rare and exquisite person as Miss Millworth has inspired a zealously protective affection in anyone's heart. It is her nature, I believe."

"What a perfectly lovely thing to say," cooed Ellen, blushing prettily. "You see, don't you Arabella, that everything is quite all right?"

"I believe I *do* see," Arabella murmured. Sir James spared her a quick, sharp glance before turning his attention so completely to Ellen that the girl looked positively giddy within moments. Arabella allowed herself to be shut out without any objection, easing away from the couple unnoticed.

CHAPTER 7

Lady Arabella attempted valiantly to distract herself from the cloud of doubt and confusion that so persistently hung over her head. Was she actually envious of her best friend's love? Surely not. Surely, she was not so shallow a person as to begrudge her friend's happiness. The bright lights and noisy chatter grated terribly on her nerves; however, and Arabella found herself escaping to the relative peace of an alcove after a particularly tedious dance partner left her wishing she were Daphne and could kick someone; most notably her most recent dance partner who had managed to step repeatedly upon her toes.

Perhaps she had been inclined to distrust Sir James Randall, simply from Ellen's accounting of their romance, she reflected, and she could not entirely rule out the humiliating possibility that mere envy was clouding her perception of the situation. But all the same, she could not rid herself of the conviction that Sir James was not all that he seemed.

Lost in thought, Arabella realized that the announcement of engagement was about to be made. Things were certainly moving on apace, but perhaps she felt so left behind because the family had been in Bath during Ellen's whirlwind courtship. Sir James Randall stood near the Millworth family, and Mr. Millworth was clearing his throat gruffly in preparation to speak. No matter what her personal feelings might be on the matter, Arabella would never dream of hurting Ellen by missing the announcement, so she rose from her partially hidden seat and moved toward her friend.

Her progress towards the main crowd was halted abruptly, however, by the sight of a gentleman standing apart from everyone else. *If gentleman were the correct term*, she thought with some confusion. Unless her eyes were playing tricks on her, Arabella was seeing the very same farm laborer that Daphne had befriended earlier that day. He could certainly not be mistaken for a laborer any longer.

He wore a stunning white waistcoat with gold threaded peacocks embroidered upon it and a dove gray superfine jacket that clung to his muscled torso. She realized that he was dressed in exquisitely tailored clothes that suited the occasion perfectly. He had, however, looked more comfortable and at ease, and a great deal happier in his shirtsleeves, with sweat dampening and darkening his blonde hair and a pile of splintered boards at his feet, she reflected.

But casting back in her memory, Arabella realized that he had not actually been dressed in the rough-spun costume of a farm hand and had never introduced himself as such to her. It had all been a matter of context and assumption, she supposed. He was not a farm laborer. She had been mistaken. The thought made her heart leap quite uncharacteristically in her chest. Since he was obviously, a gentleman of some regard, who was he?

The mystery of the stranger would not have held her interest much longer, not when competing with such an important moment in her best friend's life, at least, if Arabella had not noticed a sudden change in his expression. He had been gazing abstractedly around at the gathered gentry with very little evident interest. In fact, he had looked like nothing so much as a man who was counting the seconds until he could decently excuse himself from a party, which he had no desire to attend. He was not the only gentleman so inclined when faced with social niceties, Arabella thought. However, when Mr. Millworth began to speak, the gentleman's attention was drawn to the Millworths and Sir James Randall.

Instantly, his entire bearing changed, and Arabella felt certain that it was due to the sight of Sir James. The expression that suddenly twisted the man's handsome features spoke of recognition and intense, almost violent dislike. Indeed, Arabella noted that his hands had actually curled into fists for a moment, and he had taken a step towards the group with a dark glint in his stormy eyes before he seemed to recall his surroundings and forced himself to relax.

Arabella hastily made her way closer to her friend, to ensure that Ellen would see her applauding the announcement with all appearance of happiness, but her mind was suddenly made up. It wasn't only her imagination, or jealousy, or even her own insistence on propriety that made her take such an instant dislike to Sir James Randall. She had seen her own feelings both mirrored and magnified in the stranger's eyes, and that was somehow all the confirmation that she needed.

Looking at Mr. and Mrs. Millworth she could see that their kindly, good-hearted souls were perhaps a bit bewildered by the rapidity of their daughter's engagement, but they seemed to suspect nothing was amiss. It would be hard to feel suspicious, Arabella supposed, if one only looked at Ellen's radiant, undeniable happiness. She looked positively smitten, her eyes seeking those of her fiancé as if he were the only person in the room.

Sir James Randall was putting on a good show of being besotted and in love, Arabella thought, but she was certain that it *was* a show. There was a smugness about his smile and a coldness in his eyes that no amount of refined, handsome elegance could mask. Something was decidedly wrong about the man, and the entire situation. With this thought, Arabella decided she was going to do her best to keep Ellen from coming to disaster.

She also decided the strange laborer turned gentleman was going to be her ally in that endeavor although the mystery man did not yet know it. If nothing else, he would tell her what had put the look of disgust on his face when he looked at Sir James Randall. She was sure that if she could at least deduce the answer to that question, she might be one step closer to discovering the root of her sense of unease about Sir James Randall.

Having applauded and congratulated the couple properly, Arabella meant to slip back into the background and find some opportunity of having a word with the mystery man. She was only just in time, however, to see him hurrying out of the room with a haste that she could not hope to overcome.

"Lady Etheridge? Who was that tall gentleman who was standing over there? He left only just now," Arabella asked a passing acquaintance. It was fortunate that Lady Etheridge happened to be on the spot, really Providential, Arabella reflected privately. The stout, matronly woman was a notorious gossip and would doubtless have more information on the stranger than the man himself.

"Who, Lord Willingham? Oh, dear me, Lady Arabella, don't tell me you've developed a taste for that wicked gentleman!" Lady Etheridge gasped with delight at the very idea. "He *is* very handsome, I won't deny it, but the shocking things one hears! He is positively depraved if half of the stories can be believed."

"Really? Do you think him handsome? I couldn't tell with the frightful scowl on his face," Arabella lied hastily and unblushingly. Perhaps it had not been so Providential to seek Lady Etheridge just then after all. The woman was all but trembling with the excitement at the prospect of new gossip to spread and Arabella needed none of that. Indeed, the woman's mass of lavender ruffles and flounces was fluttering distractingly.

"His expression was what made me notice him. He looked a trifle murderous during the announcement of Miss Millworth's engagement and it made me curious," Arabella said.

"Oh, did he, *indeed*?" breathed Lady Etheridge, and Arabella saw that she had succeeded in distracting the scandal- monger's focus away from herself. "Well, I suppose that's as much as we might expect from a fortune hunting rogue such as Lord Willingham. You could hardly think the man would rejoice at there being one less eligible and wealthy beauty in his hunting grounds. I must say, this Sir Randall has certainly snapped up our dear Ellen with all possible haste."

"Did Lord Willingham have designs on Miss Millworth himself?" queried Arabella cautiously.

"Well now, he *must* have, in a general sort of way. We all know he's only stayed on that shabby little farm of his in order to snare some poor, unsuspecting girl with a dowry that can refill his coffers. I can't say that I ever heard of him showing any *particular* interest, though," admitted Lady Etheridge begrudgingly. "He can hardly have expected to compete with Sir Randall, though, not in looks *or* in fortune." Arabella disagreed with that sentiment, but she did not comment.

"Sir Randall certainly looks a bit dazzling," Arabella laughed lightly. Not for worlds would she have betrayed her true feelings on the subject of Sir James to Lady Etheridge. "Of course, I daresay most gentlemen, Lord Willingham included, could make a better showing of themselves besides him if they were smiling even a little bit."

"He is really quite handsome, *I* think. I've no doubt he will be showering all of his charm on you soon enough, dear, and you will be able to judge his smile for yourself."

"On me? I cannot see why," protested Arabella.

"Why naturally, Lady Arabella. You and your sisters will certainly come to his attention. The Sedgewicks are the best prospects in the neighborhood. Your father's title, as well as his wealth, is sure to turn Lord Willingham's head, and with dear little Ellen engaged, there is no one else with any coin to spend on the run-down farm that he is calling his estate. I'm telling you, watch your step, my dear.

"I shall. I suppose it is fortunate that I have always been so light on my feet," Arabella returned, smiling. "I can assure you I have no intention of being ensnared by any rogues or fortune- hunters, Lady Etheridge."

"One never does, my dear," Lady Etheridge shook her head, clearly enjoying her gloomy forebodings. "One never does. And yet, such things happen quite frequently, you know."

"Excuse me, won't you? I must go speak to Mr. and Mrs. Millworth," Arabella said.

"Oh, they must be perfectly delighted at their sweet Ellen making such a brilliant match, as I am sure you are yourself," Lady Etheridge said. "She is your particular friend, of course."

"Oh yes, perfectly delighted," Arabella murmured to Lady Etheridge's back as the woman bustled away importantly.

What were the odds, she wondered, frowning slightly, that the only person who seemed to share her mistrust and dislike of Sir James was also the only person with whom her father had forbidden her from associating? Arabella could scarcely recall a time when she had gone against her father's wishes, even unintentionally. He would be terribly displeased, she knew, to discover that both she and Daphne had spoken to Lord Willingham, no matter how briefly. Daphne's meeting was a spur-of-the-moment thing. It could be passed off as accidental, but what she was planning…

Arabella considered her options. No one else seemed to mind Sir James at all. Were they all so taken in with his charm? Did no one sense anything amiss? There was only Lord Christopher…

Lord Ashbury would probably never find out about Daphne's accidental meeting—certainly her sister was unlikely to mention it to him—but Arabella wondered just how much further her luck would hold if she chose to intentionally defy the earl's wishes.

※

Christopher threw himself moodily into his saddle, grateful that he had decided to ride to the assembly at the Millworth home rather than take a more conventional carriage. He had suspected he wouldn't care for the tedium of a carriage ride after the still worse tedium of the evening, which he had only barely forced himself to attend. It would have been much better if he had stayed home and risked being labeled a recluse as well as a scoundrel, for he could imagine nothing that could have put him in a worse temper than the sight of Sir James Randall beaming at that collection of fools.

Of all the out-of-the-way little villages in England, it was maddening to discover that the most unconscionable scoundrel of his acquaintance had invaded *his* particular village, Christopher reflected bitterly. Not that he could truly lay claim to the place, considering how reviled he was, but public opinion could not change the fact that it was his home.

It was ridiculous that a villain such as Sir James could be so readily and freely accepted by the same gathering that would hardly spare a civil word for him. And to see that villain smirking beside that poor, innocent girl, receiving congratulations and well-wishes on his engagement! He wanted to pop the fellow right there in the ballroom. Christopher urged his horse into a gallop, wishing he could outpace his own futile frustration. Perhaps, Sir James actually meant to marry this time, although Christopher could hardly credit the idea, knowing what he did. It would really be worse luck for the hapless Miss Millworth if he did.

There was nothing he could do, regardless, and that thought rankled terribly. It wasn't as if the matter was any of his business, particularly with the way the Millworths had made a point of sweeping their daughter away from him in horror any time he chanced to encounter the family. The last few such interactions had been sufficient to convince him that his best course of action would be to avoid the eligible young ladies of the community at all costs, to avoid riling up an angry mob of suspicious parents.

He would bide his time. Breed his horses and refill his coffers. If by that time, he was not accepted by the town, he would move on. Willowbrook Farm of course, was not entailed. He could sell it at will, unlike the worthless piece of property that was the barony. That land and the people upon it were a drain on his nonexistent finances. He needed to concentrate on his horses and the new breeding program until he had a few coins to rub together. He need not give a fig about the Millworth girl and Randall. For all he knew, they deserved one another.

There was no satisfaction, however, in the idea that the Millworths had failed utterly to recognize the real threat to their child's happiness. No amount of ill treatment could make Christopher rejoice in someone else's suffering. No one ever did seem to recognize the danger of Sir James Randall until it was far too late. The man had fooled a great many people far more wise and worldly than the sheltered and rural Millworths. In any case, there was nothing he could do about it, no matter how it galled him to let the man live and breathe in gentle society.

CHAPTER 8

Arabella had succeeded in avoiding her sisters when she and their father returned home from the Millfords. Daphne had been very pointedly not speaking to her, and had only stayed up so late to make sure that Arabella noticed she was being ignored. Rather than attempt to cajole the child into forgetting her ill humor with apologies, promises of treats, and outright bribery as Daphne expected, Arabella had disregarded the silent treatment altogether.

"Not speaking to me? Well that certainly simplifies matters," she said. "I've had rather plenty of excitement for one evening and I'm longing for my bed. I'll tell you all about it in the morning, Marianne, and Daphne you can listen in if you care to hear the news. If not, well, so be it. Goodnight!"

As she breezed up the staircase, Arabella heard the crash of a porcelain vase being hurled against the wall but did not so much as pause or flinch at the sound. It was almost as satisfying as if she had thrown it herself.

"Good Heavens, child, have you taken leave of your senses?" Lord Ashbury demanded, sounding more astonished than he had any right to be at the display of temper. Had he never taken *any* notice of Daphne's tantrums, Arabella wondered with some asperity as she continued up the staircase, her father's chiding voice in her ears.

More than anything, Arabella had wanted to be alone with her thoughts, to have a few uninterrupted hours during which time she might attempt to sift through all of her mental confusion. There was no chance of sleep, she was certain, considering how agitated her sensibilities were. She had every intention of lying awake in her bed for the remainder of the night and was shocked to find herself waking in the morning, full sunlight streaming onto her pillow.

"I thought that might rouse you," Marianne remarked from beside the window, busily tying back the heavy brocade draperies she had evidently just drawn back. "I wanted to let you rest as long as possible, of course, but you've slept through breakfast and as noon draws closer, I am becoming more than a little afraid that *two* unsupervised meals in a row may result in a small outbreak of violence."

"I never sleep so late!" exclaimed Arabella, bolting upright in her bed. "How singularly strange. I thought I would be unable to sleep a wink and instead I slept more deeply than I can ever remember doing. I am wonderfully refreshed, too."

"I am glad to hear it. My sacrifice hasn't been in vain," laughed Marianne. "Actually, it wasn't such a very difficult sacrifice, after all. I thought I would have to mediate all manner of hideous arguments over breakfast in your absence, but really, I think Daphne and Father are both feeling rather too baffled to lose their tempers again after last night's row. It won't last, I'm sure, and I would rather not be alone when one or the other of them regains a sense of balance."

"It'll be Daphne first, I'll warrant," said Arabella decisively, swinging her feet out from under the bedclothes with great energy. "Father is too used to retreating into his books and papers, whereas Daphne hasn't the proper amount of focus to stay confused for very long at a time. She will simply refuse to think about whatever is perplexing her and throw herself into something else entirely. I *am* sorry to have left you to deal with it all on your own, though." Arabella pushed her feet into slippers and wrapped her robe around her.

"Oh, it's good for me; for all of us, I daresay. You never saw anything so funny as Father's face last night when he saw Daphne shatter that vase. Unless it was Daphne's face when you refused to take any notice of her. Father chided her for a good quarter hour over care and costs. My own eyes glazed over," Marianne admitted.

"It will be well if Father does not learn of the loss of the dress," Arabella said thinking of the beautiful silk melting in the flames.

"Or perhaps he should," mused Marianne. "Poor Letty sifted through the ashes to find the silver thread. It's nothing but a lump of silver and tiny silver strands. Certainly, it is no longer silver thread. I'm not sure what is to be done with it."

"Where is Letty?" Arabella wondered why the maid was not here to attend her.

"Her mother was ill. I told her that she could have the day off. Dora and I would manage without her."

Arabella shrugged uncertain herself as she thought of the ruined dress. She continued unbraiding the plait that she had put her hair in for sleep. Unfortunately, most of it was already out of the braid and tangled. "When you see her, tell Letty she can have the silver for her trouble. She's such a blessing to put up with us, I think."

Marianne was silent for a moment just gazing at her sister in the glass. She picked up Arabella's brush and began to brush her sister's silky hair, carefully pulling out the tangles. "Tell me. Have you just made up your mind to leave Father and Daphne to their own devices all of a sudden, Arabella?"

"I haven't made up my mind to *anything*," Arabella replied truthfully. She closed her eyes enjoying the feel of the brush gliding through her hair. "I certainly didn't upset either of them deliberately. I do feel odd, though. As if coming home last night had suddenly forced me to step outside of myself for a moment, and that moment was enough to make me realize I needed to do things differently. I didn't feel nearly so calm about it, or about anything else, before now. I really couldn't say what has changed."

"Perhaps this sudden alteration was triggered by the news of Ellen's betrothal?" Marianne suggested, her blue eyes twinkling merrily at her sister as she held the brush aloft.

"Can you ever forgive me for not telling you all about the soiree last night?" Arabella asked, wincing remorsefully, or perhaps it was because of a tangle in her hair.

"Sorry," Marianne murmured. "I should send for Dora."

"No," Arabella said, putting a hand to her hair. "It is nothing. It is just that I felt as if my emotions were all too tangled up last night. I really could not speak to anyone, not even you."

"I gathered as much, the way you sailed up the staircase the minute you returned home. Besides, I was not left in ignorance for very long. Father actually told me Ellen's news once he had finished scolding Daphne for breaking that vase."

"*Father* told you the news?" Arabella turned from the mirror and stared at her sister in abject disbelief.

"Indeed, he did! He seemed to be rather under the impression that you were not entirely delighted by the announcement that was made at the soiree and wanted to know if I could shed any light onto your discomfiture."

"I should never have dreamed that Father would notice such a thing, let alone bother about it. Indeed, Marianne,

I cannot even recall seeing him in the room when the announcement was made."

"Perhaps your attention was distracted by other things?"

"Undoubtedly it was," Arabella murmured, half to herself, thinking of the fascinating scowl on Lord Willingham's arresting face.

"But you haven't said that Father was wrong in his impression," Marianne pressed, jolting Arabella out of the surprisingly vivid memory.

"Father's impression?" Arabella was still thinking of Lord Willingham, and the earl's oddly vehement order that they have nothing to do with the man. "It may have been wrong. I can't imagine what he can have based his opinion on, after all."

"It *may* have been wrong? You sound for all the world as if you yourself do not know if you were upset by the announcement of Ellen's engagement last night or not," Marianne exclaimed, looking strangely at Arabella.

"Oh. That. I mean, no, Father was not entirely wrong," Arabella scrambled about, confusedly, and a tap came to the door.

"Come," Arabella called and Dora, Marianne's maid peeked into the room. "Letty has gone to her mother's," Dora said. "May I help you dress, my lady?"

"Yes," Arabella agreed, and Marianne gave up her brush to the maid.

"I just have some doubts as to the worthiness of that Sir James Randall, that is all. It all happened so suddenly, you know, and I suppose I cannot help feeling a little suspicious of him. He *is* charming, though. Perhaps too charming. And almost as handsome as Ellen claimed. I'm being foolish, more likely than not."

Marianne sat on the edge of the bed and watched Dora work. "A charming, handsome man who comes and sweeps a girl off of her feet? Most especially a rich girl. He sounds like a decidedly suspicious character if you ask me," Marianne teased. "But I won't go so far as to say you're being foolish over it. I am certain that I won't think any suitor is quite good enough for you, even if he meets all of your rigorous qualifications. It is natural to want absolute perfection for your loved ones, and you certainly love your friend, Ellen. I suppose it is just as natural to mistrust absolute perfection when it *does* appear."

"That is the trouble, I am sure," Arabella agreed. "And I just need a little time to come around to the idea and to get to know Sir James." She would have to find some sort of way to bear his company, she thought, but there was no sense in mentioning that to Marianne. "You know how dear Ellen is to me and she can be so romantic and impractical. I suppose I am all the more suspicious of Sir James because of that."

"Undoubtedly," Marianne agreed, although she was still looking a little askance at Arabella. "And now perhaps you will consent to join the rest of your family?"

"Of course. I will be down shortly." She turned to Dora. "I'll wear the hunter green morning dress," she said, and Dora pulled two green dresses from her closet, a question in her eyes.

"The one with the lilies embroidered on the bodice," she said indicating a short-sleeved muslin dress. "It's not too late in the year to wear the flowers, I think."

"Of course not, my lady," Dora said.

"And perhaps the matching Spenser jacket," Marianne suggested. "It is cool if you plan to go outside."

Marianne left the bed chamber, and Dora, continued to assist Arabella in dressing. Arabella scarcely registered the maid's presence, so absorbed was she in her thoughts. Her unexpectedly restful night's sleep, seemed to have clarified her feelings without any conscious input, and she felt more certain than ever that Sir James Randall boded no good for her friend. She was sure that she must put a stop to the engagement before any more harm could come to Ellen, but what could she, as a woman, do? How could she find any reason to stop the marriage, if that is what she should do? Upon introspection, she determined she needed a gentleman's help.

What was more, she was more determined than ever to enlist the assistance of Lord Willingham. At least, she needed to find out what he knew about the man. She was sure he knew something about Sir James. Her actions would mean defying her father's express wishes, but after all, Arabella reasoned as the maid skillfully and silently arranged her hair, who better to thwart a suspected rake than an even worse rake? Besides, who would he tell the plan? As far as she could see, no one in town was speaking to him. Now, she only had to find a way to conveniently meet him and speak to him on the subject.

CHAPTER 9

Christopher decided that he had had enough of local Society. They did not know him, and he did not care to know them. Instead of attending events, he buckled down and concentrated on completing the stable. He was focused on the work and had made a lot of progress in the past week.

The late afternoon tended toward briskness as he bid farewell to his foreman and surveyed the progress of the restoration with a small burst of satisfaction. It was still warm, but autumn was in the air and he knew he would have few nice days before the rain came. The past few days had been busy. A drainage ditch was dug to keep the rain water from coming into the stalls, when the inevitable rain came, and ten wide square birthing stalls were laid with smooth dirt floors and stout boards. On either side of the stable, a good distance from one another were large stalls for two stallions with solid latches. Smaller stalls for the geldings and mares not in foal were in various stages of repair. The stables would be safe and sturdy and functional once again with new life breathed into them. Not that he had ever really doubted it, but Christopher knew that both his workers and his neighbors had considered the undertaking to be rather mad. He still had plans for the tack rooms and a business office and other niceties to come, but the stables would be ready for inhabitants by the end of the month, which was really an impressive feat. With any luck, he could have a stallion and several mares in foal before winter arrived. That meant of course, that he would have to continue to live above the kitchen in the servants' quarters, but at least it was warm and dry and did not stink of mildew.

His brief moment of contentment was shattered, however, by the appearance of a particular young lady on horseback. Christopher allowed himself the quick indulgence of a muttered curse before resignedly moving to greet the strangely persistent and eminently beautiful Lady Arabella Sedgewick.

The annoying creature had seemingly dogged his footsteps every time he ventured from his farm for the past week, and had developed an uncanny instinct regarding his whereabouts. He had not left Willowbend for the past two days, so determined was he to avoid her ever since she had practically forced an introduction on the church steps.

He would never have guessed her capable of such behavior, not the icy, reserved young lady who had unwillingly followed a spirited little sister onto his land the week before. *She* had looked at him as though he were a particularly revolting specimen of monster, one whom she could not get away from quickly enough. Yet now, she seemed to seek his company. He could not divine her motives, and such mysteries were an anathema to him. He liked things straightforward and plain. This woman was neither of these two things. Besides, she was the daughter of the Earl of Ashbury, a person he should avoid at all costs. And he thought, she should want to avoid him too. What was her purpose? And how had she changed so completely from wanting nothing to do with him, to seeking him out at every turn?. He had to suspect some ulterior motive.

"Why, good afternoon, Baron Willingham," Arabella called brightly, cantering up to him with a pleased expression on her glorious face, as though delighted at a purely accidental meeting with an old friend. Her hair was falling from the chignon which caught it at the nape of her neck. She looked thoroughly disheveled and quite lovely. Bella, he thought. Her very name meant beautiful. Her color was high. He wondered if she rode hard to get here. Perhaps that was to lose the attention of a groom which undoubtedly should have been accompanying her.

"Lady Arabella, surely you can't be affecting surprise at finding me here, on my own land," Christopher replied gruffly. If the girl would insist on pursuing his company, then he saw no reason to make any pretense of good manners. It was best if she left directly.

"No, indeed," she laughed, unabashed. "I am not affecting anything, I assure you, sir," she said as she tucked back a stray lock of hair that had come loose, no doubt during her ride. I came here with no other purpose than to speak with you, and I won't waste either of our time by pretending otherwise. "Won't you help me dismount?" She tucked a stray hair under her riding bonnet.

When asked so bluntly, he could not refuse without being rude. He came forward and looped the reins of the horse over his arm, while reaching up to lift her from the saddle. He did not notice the fine silk of her hair in her eyes. He tried very hard not to notice petite perfection of her waist as his hands nearly spanned it. He did not breathe deeply of her perfume, nor did he note her small warm hands on his chest, balancing herself as he put her feet on the ground. He released her and immediately stepped back out of the range of her feminine wiles, or at least he attempted the same. How had she gone from castigating her sister for speaking to him, to seeking him out so relentlessly?

Well, perhaps there really were such things as changelings, Christopher reflected, but wasn't that supposed to be children, not grown women? She certainly was a woman grown. Her attitude had indeed altered in the past week. In his own previous life, he would not have avoided making the acquaintance of such a stunningly beautiful woman, let alone actively fleeing from her, but many things had changed since his uncle's death.

"I must say, I am quite genuine in my surprise at actually finding you, as you have been running from me all week," she said as she tucked several locks of hair beneath her bonnet.

"I would hardly say *running*," Christopher objected, stung by the implication that he was frightened of her. He was annoyed to find himself securing her horse, when he wanted her to ride away more than anything.

"Avoiding, then. Or whatever term best suits you, it's all the same to me," Arabella was carelessly agreeable, and not particularly concerned with Christopher's discomfort.

Standing on the ground she had to look up quite a way to meet his eyes, and she did so a little mockingly, her lips quirking in a strangely alluring way. "I can scarcely blame you, as I have been quite shockingly bold and persistent. Anyone who knows me could tell you that such behavior is very unlike my typical character. But you see, Lord Willingham, I want something very badly and I believe you are the only man who can give it to me."

The innuendo sent an immediate fire through his blood. No changeling this, but a flesh and blood woman who was eminently desirable, but that could not be what she meant. She was a lady, through and through, and more so, regardless to what the Ton or the current town might conjecture, he was a gentleman.

"Whatever you have heard of my reputation, madam," Christopher began, drawing himself up in shock and embarrassment. He paused; his discomfort only increased when the infuriating creature stared blankly at him for a moment and then burst into a peal of delighted, musical laughter.

"Oh dear, I suppose I have expressed myself badly," Arabella managed after a moment, composing herself. "If I have given you the impression that I am applying to you for some sort of scandal. That isn't at *all* what I mean, Lord Willingham. Although, if I were to accept the things I *have* heard of your reputation, I should be a bit surprised you would object to accommodating me. I am generally considered to be reasonably attractive, you know." She tilted her head, and he noticed that regardless of her attention, her hair was again falling in the most enchanting disarray. He wanted to take the bonnet from her head and free the silken strands from their captivity.

The woman was far more than reasonably attractive. She was breathtakingly beautiful, and more than that, she had the self-possession of a woman rather than the silly foibles of the girls who seemed to come out each year. Was it possible that they were younger and younger, or was he just getting older, he wondered? He shook his head and demanded, "Whatever do you want from me?" Christopher refused to acknowledge her teasing. "I cannot imagine any way in which I might be of assistance to you, Lady Arabella. My reputation, as you say, is not one that commends me to my neighbors, and I do my best to keep out of the way of young ladies because I do not wish to rouse public indignation any further. You know what gossip in a small village is, doubtless. If you wish to court scandal in order to annoy your father or make some lazy suitor jealous, then I wish you would do so without involving myself. I am not interested."

"I've already said that I want nothing of the sort from you," Arabella said, looking curiously at Christopher. "As a matter of fact, what I need has really nothing to do with myself. I just happened to notice last week, at the Millworth's soiree, the way that you were looking at Sir James Randall when his engagement to Miss Millworth was announced."

Whatever he might have guessed or expected the young lady to say, it had not remotely been that. Christopher fairly gaped at her for a moment before gathering composure. He picked up a spate of sandpaper and began absently rubbing the stall door with it to collect his thoughts. He paused long enough to check the door for splinters before answering. He had hoped to garner his thoughts. He assumed that perhaps the lady might grow bored, but she sat patiently awaiting his reply.

"And how, precisely, do you imagine I was looking at Sir Randall?" he asked cautiously.

"As if you wanted to wrap your hands around his neck, and choke the life from him," replied Arabella quite coolly. She brushed back another stray lock of hair with her gloved hand.

Christopher spun to look at her.

"I happened to be looking at you rather just as your attention was drawn to him, so you needn't bother denying it. Your dislike for that gentleman was quite plain for a moment, before you managed to mask it."

"I don't suppose I ought to be surprised that a young lady as bold and persistent as yourself would be embarrassed to admit she had been staring at a strange man," hedged Christopher, wanting to avoid the subject of his hatred of Sir Randall if possible. He went back to sanding the door although it was already quite smooth and splinter free.

"If anyone heard you describe me in such terms, they would most undoubtedly laugh in your face," Arabella said without so much as a blush. "I have quite a reputation for being almost perfectly correct and proper in all of my interactions."

"Yet another case for the idea that most reputations have decidedly little to do with actual character," the man muttered not looking at her.

"As for my reasons for looking at you closely at the Assembly, I should think that would be perfectly obvious," she said as she stripped off her riding gloves and perched herself on the only seat in the barn, a small round stool, her gloves placed neatly in her lap. "I have no doubt that you knew I mistook you for a common farm hand when my younger sister and I blundered onto your property the other day. I was rather taken aback to see you make an appearance, dressed as a gentleman, at Millworth House as anyone might be."

"Indeed," Christopher muttered picking up a hammer and putting it back down again. He couldn't quite bring himself to be so rude as to continue his work. He had run away from her for long enough. Instead, he finally adjusted his shirt sleeves so as to cover his bare arms and faced her squarely. He noted that Lady Arabella's eyes followed the movement and then determinedly looked at his face, the heat of a blush rising along her cheeks, a single hair unattended as it clung to her lips.

"But that is all incidental," she continued, "as I am sure you realize. I have been seeking, boldly and persistently, as you say, a chance to speak with you ever since because I was so struck by the loathing in your expression when you regarded Sir Randall. I want to know why you dislike him. Your particular reasons, I mean."

"My particular reasons for disliking anyone can have little value to you," he retorted, rather rudely. "Certainly, I am entitled to like or dislike whomever I please without it being a matter of public record, although everything else I do seem to draw the attention of the town. I am doing my best to keep out of gossip and petty squabbles. You surely must have noticed that I am reviled enough in this village as it is without adding to the fodder."

"If this were a matter of simply nosiness or a petty squabble, you can't imagine that I would risk my reputation by seeking a gentleman of *your* reputation out so determinedly," Arabella snapped, losing patience. "I require information about Sir Randall because I wish to confirm my own suspicions about him, namely that the man is a scoundrel and untrustworthy."

"Why?" he ventured.

She sucked in a deep breath, and Christopher felt the sincerity of her words. "Baron Willingham, Miss Ellen Millworth is my dearest and oldest friend, and her happiness means a great deal to me, enough to risk damaging my own reputation and defying my father. I believe, you can tell me more about Randall's past and his character. Things that I, as a woman would have no recourse to discover. And so, I have sought you out. Am I mistaken in my supposition?"

"You are not mistaken," Christopher replied heavily after a long moment that all but sang with tension. "Not about the fact that I can tell you at least something of Sir Randall's past and character, nor are you wrong about the fact that I despise him quite fiercely, nor again in your idea that he is untrustworthy." Christopher shook his head and then turned to face her. "How on Earth did you come to guess that, though? Randall tends to charm everyone he meets, particularly young ladies."

"I suppose 'guess' is the best explanation," admitted Arabella. "I felt suspicious to begin with, when Miss Millworth confided in me that she had been secretly corresponding with Sir James Randall all summer. She is her parents' only child, and well loved. She has no reason to hold this correspondence from them. They would give Helen her heart's desire. That said, I also love her dearly, but I can say that she is a romantic, dreamy sort; quite ready to be swept off of her feet, you know."

"And that is just Randall's favorite type of conquest, I am afraid. Well, adding in the facts that she is a beautiful and wealthy girl, of course."

"A fortune hunting scoundrel's ideal mark, I should imagine," Arabella interjected with an arch look at Christopher.

"I wouldn't know anything about it," he retorted stiffly.

"Well, beyond my initial suspicion of the way the affair was conducted, I can only tell you that I took an immediate dislike to Sir James. There is something about his manner that seems false, something that makes me uncomfortable. He may *look* like a golden demigod," here Christopher gave an ungentlemanly snort, making Arabella smile. "But there is an ugliness to him that I can't quite define, and I certainly can't ignore. You aren't going to tell me that you think he will make a good husband for my sweet friend, are you?"

"I won't tell you anything of the sort. Randall wouldn't make a suitable husband for any decent woman, or any indecent woman, for that matter."

"Indeed!" Arabella drew her breath in sharply and felt a blush rise to her cheeks at the indelicacy of Lord Willingham's comment.

"Lady Arabella, this is not an acceptable topic for me to discuss with you, and I cannot claim to have either the skill or the patience to couch everything in polite and vague terms. This matter is not one that is fit for delicate ears," Christopher said bluntly. "But you have come to me for my opinion, and I will not sugar coat it."

"Yes, I see that," Arabella said slowly, nodding her head. Her bonnet unexpectedly fell sideways from her head. "Oh, bother," she said as she attempted to right it. She continued unabashed. "I also appreciate your plain speaking, Lord Willingham. You must forgive my reactions if I seem scandalized, for as bold as I doubtless appear to you, I am actually moving quite beyond my depth in this, but for a friend, I must persevere."

"Certainly," he agreed shortly. He was quickly developing a begrudging admiration for Lady Arabella's courage and devotion to her friend but he was in no mood to encourage her by saying so. "Here now, I am not about to invite you unchaperoned into my home so that my housekeeper may spread a new scandal about the village within a quarter of an hour's time, but there is no reason to keep standing while we talk. There is a small pavilion over by the pond and it is reasonably sturdy if you would care to have a seat in it. You might be more comfortable, and we can talk."

"Yes, thank you," said Arabella, rather meekly. The enormity of the risks she was taking had suddenly struck her afresh, dimming her satisfaction at having finally acquired the confirmation from Lord Willingham that she had been seeking all week.

He removed her horse's bridal and put the mare in one of the finished stalls. Then he escorted her the short walk to the pavilion, which was a rustic and rather charming spot in spite of its state of disrepair. Overgrown with hanging wisteria vines, the old stone structure was quite hidden from view, not that Christopher had very many servants about the premises to see them anyhow.

They walked in silence, which lingered for a few strange minutes after they had taken seats in the sheltering gloom of the pavilion. Christopher was struck with the sudden privacy and realized that if he were the rake that the town accused him of being, the Lady Arabella had wandered unwittingly into his trap.

"Are you always so trusting?" he asked.

"No," she said impatiently shoving a stray hair behind her ear and knocking her bonnet more askew. "But I consider myself a good judge of character. That is why I must know the truth about Randall. I must satisfy myself that I am right about him." She shoved another hair out of her face with a sound of annoyance.

Without thinking, he reached up and caught the hair that she was trying to push back out of her face, smoothing it back, and then, with sudden abandon, he untied the bonnet and removed it from her head. Beneath it, her hair had come loose from its chignon and was in complete disarray. Lud, she was beautiful. He wanted to run his hands through the silky strands and bury his face in its sweet perfume.

She sucked in a hesitating breath, her eyes wide, but she did not move from his touch. He loosened a pin and secured a lock here and there. He secured another that had come unloosened from the chignon until her coif was neat. Her hair in his hands felt like liquid fire, and when she tipped her head up, he was nearly undone.

Instead of kissing her, he thumbed another stray hair from her lips, and pinned it. Then he carefully placed the bonnet back on her head and tied it to the left of her chin.

"How did you…" she began, and then thought better of whatever she was going to say, but he could complete the thought. She was wondering when he learned to secure a lady's hair, so expertly, so quickly. She blushed profusely, and he could have eased her embarrassment with two words—five sisters. But he said nothing. He only raised an eyebrow. He expected her to run. She did not. She only swallowed; her eyes were the deepest blue he had ever seen as she looked into his.

"Thank you," she said primly.

CHAPTER 10

Everything in Arabella was shouting at her to run. This man that she had befriended was a rake. Everyone had said so, and yet, she strangely trusted him, even when he had secured her hair with warm, sure fingers. Fingers, she told herself that had obviously done this before, which begged the question: What lady had he put back to rights, and how had that lady become disheveled? Was it so innocent an encounter as her own? She doubted it.

The man was well-known as a rake. She could barely breathe with the knowledge. It seemed as if the cool breeze had sucked all the air from her lungs. Her father had warned her against this man. The town gossiped about his ill deeds. Why did his touch bring such riotous thoughts to the fore? She could not trust him, but for her friend, she had to find out what he knew about Randall.

He sat now with his hands in his lap—his large careful hands—hands that had touched her. She had wanted to lean into that touch, but she did not dare. She swallowed the fire that seemed to bubble up from somewhere within her, and cleared her throat. Her hands were shaking, and she felt deliciously warm. How was it that she felt warm when the air was decidedly cool? Perhaps it was the sun, she convinced herself. At last, she spoke.

She hoped her voice did not tremble, but she feared it did. "I—I do appreciate you speaking to me, Lord Willingham," Arabella said, forcing herself to break the silence, a little awkwardly. "I can assure you that I won't breathe a word of our conversation to anyone. I won't do anything to make your position here any more difficult than it already is."

"I would appreciate that, greatly," he said. "There has been enough gossip about me since my uncle's death to last me a lifetime." He gave a small shrug. "I suppose I can count on your silence, as it serves in your own best interest as well, perhaps even more than mine. You think me rude and ungracious for saying so, no doubt, but the truth of the matter is that I have no other reason to trust you, or anyone else for that matter."

"Still, it is the woman who would suffer for such gossip; not the man," she reminded him.

"I know that is so, but still you persist. You are a tenacious woman."

"Yes. I must be so for my friend's sake, and I know, there is no reason for you to be gracious with someone who is insisting on forcing a conversation that you do not care to have," she replied evenly.

Lord Willingham looked away and Arabella urged him to continue. "As I said earlier, I appreciate your speaking plainly to me even if it is a trifle unusual."

"Well, to speak plainly, then," Lord Willingham said, clearing his throat uncomfortably. "I may say that it comes as a surprise to me that Randall has entered into a formal agreement with your friend. The fact is, I have never known him to actually go so far as to commit himself to a lady's hand."

"But wouldn't that be the entire point of, well, of being a fortune hunter?" wondered Arabella, knitting her brow in concentration.

"Ah, well, in one sense yes. But until this point, I understand that the matches he would have been pleased to make all fell through for one reason or another. He has made rather a name for himself as a general sort of scoundrel in certain circles. He has had a good deal of success in the past three or so years supplementing his income with gambling and other, less savory activities, shall we say."

"What sort of activities?" Arabella, when she saw he seemed hesitant to answer her, added. "Lord Willingham, I really must learn what I am dealing with if I am to be of any real service to my friend, you know."

"Very well. I can say that I know of several instances where Sir Randall has seduced a wealthy, married lady and then extorted money from her in exchange for his continued discretion."

"He truly is a scoundrel, then!" exclaimed Arabella, feeling sick at the idea of sweet, affectionate Ellen falling into the clutches of such a monstrous person. She did her best to school her expression into neutral lines, but it was difficult to not feel a little horrified that she was sitting beside a man who had kept such company.

"Of the worst kind, in my opinion," Lord Willingham replied, and then added, as if guessing at her thoughts. "I daresay you won't believe me. You have no reason to, but for all of my sins, I have never associated with Randall or any of his ilk. I know him because he was a frequent companion of my late uncle's these past few years."

"The uncle from whom you have inherited your title?"

"Title and reputation, unfortunately. It has occurred to me quite a few times in the past few months that I cannot say for certain that the one is worth the other.

"The barony is in ruin. The entailed house is in even worse condition than Willowbrook Farm. It sits on an unfertile rock in the middle of nowhere, and the surrounding lands which might have brought an income have all been sold, so there is little to support the barony unless I make good with my knowledge of horses. That at least my uncle taught me, although that was not by design."

"Did your uncle deserve his reputation, I wonder?"

"What makes you say that?"

"It strikes me that in spite of all the talk I have heard since my family returned home from Bath, no one has been able to say a single wicked deed that *you* have definitely committed, Lord Willingham. Was your uncle the same?"

"I can assure you, my Uncle John was no saint," Christopher replied in a bitter, cynical tone.

Oddly enough, Arabella realized that the very fact that Lord Willingham did not take the opportunity to protest the blamelessness of his uncle's character made her more inclined to trust him about his own.

"I suppose he hardly can have been a saint, if he was friends with a man like Sir James," she ventured after a moment.

"I do not say they were friends, madam, but companions. I suspected Randall was one of the key reasons for my uncle's final descent into utter dissolution—he somehow encouraged wilder behavior than even my wicked uncle had previously indulged in, and my uncle had nothing like the strength of character required to resist the temptations that Sir Randall constantly dangled before him."

"And that is why you hate Sir Randall so desperately? Because you felt he contributed to the destruction of your uncle?"

"I did not know my uncle well enough for that, if you want the unadorned truth, Lady Arabella," Christopher answered, meeting her level gaze. "And there were plenty of other 'gentlemen' that Uncle John associated with, who were nearly as wicked as Sir James Randall, and who encouraged my uncle's ultimate destruction as well. Living here in Northwickshire, you must know of them at least by gossip. Although, I do not generally speak ill of the dead, the Baron Shudley and the late Duke of Bramblewood come to mind."

She frowned in confusion. "I do not usually give much mind to gossip," she said.

"Undoubtedly, or you would not be here," he said. He took a breath and continued. "No, I have another reason altogether for my hatred of Randall. You have shown yourself to be remarkably insightful. Perhaps you can guess it."

"Have I?" Arabella was surprised to hear herself described so, particularly by her unsociable and reluctant companion. Her own father did not seem to know her so well. How was it that this man was able to see her for who she really was? She looked into Christopher's piercing blue eyes and felt for a moment as if she could see into his very soul. Perhaps he felt the same. It was almost as if they had known one another through time itself. It made her feel strange, and a little giddy.

She paused before she spoke. "Well, if I were to guess, knowing that you do not hate Sir James because he encouraged your uncle down a harmful path, then I might imagine that he had harmed someone else. Someone more innocent or defenseless than your uncle. Perhaps, someone for whom you cared deeply."

"Right again," he said, shaking his head a little.

"Someone you loved?" she murmured.

He shook his head. "Not in the way you imagine, but close enough, I suppose. Though I was not in love with the young lady, but I did feel a certain brotherly regard. She was a friend of my youngest sister, Lydia."

"You have sisters?" she questioned.

"Five of them," he admitted ruefully. "They are with their aunt."

Arabella raised an eyebrow.

"Not my Uncle John's widow," he corrected. "My maternal Aunt Jenny. In any case, besides Sarah being friends with Lydia, she was in turn, the younger sister of a friend of mine, a friend who was a fool for ever allowing someone like Randall to meet with his sister for even a half of a second." Lord Willingham's eyes burned with passion, and Arabella once again felt the anger, just beneath the surface. There was a danger in this man, whether or not he was the rake that the village assumed him to be. She felt he would protect what was his with uncompromising sentiment if need be. He was not a man to cross.

"Apparently that is all the time Sir James needs to win a lady's heart," Arabella remarked drily, thinking of Ellen's rhapsodic tale of love at first sight.

"She was very innocent, and pretty, and young, this particular lady. Perhaps a bit foolish and romantic, as you have described your Miss Millworth to be. But she had no fortune whatsoever, and therefore Randall had no intention of ever marrying her. He was simply amusing himself, playing some sort of private game. He made her fall in love with him, not that it was a very difficult task, and somehow convinced her at the same time that no one else had ever really cared for her. It was brutal, Lady Arabella, seeing how quickly he cut her off from every friend and protector she had. Within a few weeks' time the girl hung on his every word and would listen to no one else. Even my sister, Lydia, could not get through to her; nor the girl's own brother."

"That is horrible," murmured Arabella, thinking of the besotted look on Ellen's face when she spoke of Sir James or looked at him. It had seemed merely foolish before, but now it struck Arabella as dangerous.

"My friend discovered the peril his sister was in too late, for even if her reputation could have been saved, she would not have allowed it," Lord Willingham continued, staring moodily into the distance and speaking almost as if to himself. "She ruined herself, quite willingly, a sweet innocent girl who had never so much as considered an indiscretion before meeting him. She ran away with Randall and he deserted her halfway to Gretna Green, not far from here actually. He made a point, I believe, of ensuring that what she had done was discovered, and that he looked blameless, himself, naturally."

"I hardly see how he managed to accomplish *that*," Arabella protested. She knew, of course, that society was rather harder on a ruined girl than on the scoundrel who ruined her, but all the same she had never heard of such a man not facing at least a high degree of informal censure.

"He claimed complete ignorance of the entire matter. He said he was traveling for business and when he discovered that the besotted creature had followed him, he was shocked. He left immediately, that sort of thing. He had the evidence of her own hand against her, unfortunately. He 'carelessly' left a few of her more desperate love letters lying about where a notorious scandal-monger would find them, and of course that person spread the story around Town quite enthusiastically," Lord Willingham paused in his explanation, evidently wrestling with his overwhelming dislike of gossips.

"I will say it was compelling evidence. In one letter she was actually begging him to run away with her. If I didn't know, firsthand, that she was not a wicked girl of any sort, I doubtless would have been unsympathetic myself. But you must understand this point, above all others, if you wish to help your friend. He took that innocent, pure-hearted child, for a child is really all she was, in experience if not in years—and peeled away every loyalty, every scruple, every aspect of her character, in fact. Until all that remained was her blind and all-consuming affection for him. He separated her from all who might have saved her from her folly. If I had not seen it for myself, I would not have dreamed that such a feat was humanly possible."

"The poor girl," said Arabella, unconsciously drawing her arms close for warmth. In spite of the warmth of the sun, she felt a bone-deep chill from Lord Haye's tale. It would have been a comfort if she could have disbelieved even a portion of his recitation, but every word rang with truth. "Do you know what became of her? Of course, you do."

"Why of course?" Christopher asked.

"Oh, I know nothing is ever truly 'of course' but it strikes me that you are the sort of person who would have found out, and tried to help if you could. That is all I meant."

"You are quite the student of human nature, aren't you, Lady Arabella?"

"Perhaps," Arabella had never even thought of such a thing. But maybe, she considered, one did learn at least something of the kind, through years of doggedly attempting to keep peace.

"Well, I do, of course, know what became of the poor creature. She was utterly and publicly ruined, as I have said. There was even talk of a child, but I did not press my friend for such details. It did not seem my place, but I do know my own sister was strangely subdued after the news broke.

"My friend, her brother, sent her to stay with an aunt or some such relative in the countryside near Dover to get her away from the scandal as much as he could. The worst of it was that for quite some time she could not be made to understand that she had been betrayed by Randall, so unshakable was his hold on her. She actually thought he would come for her.

"My friend was furious, but initially he thought he could persuade Randall to do the honorable thing and marry her. I went with him to that interview, and Randall laughed in his face. There was not the faintest chance, he declared, that he would consider marrying such a penniless little fool, although he said she was—well, never mind what he said. It is irrelevant." Lord Willingham's jaw tightened imperceptibly.

"He stopped pretending to be charming," noted Arabella, feeling somehow that this was important. "At least for a moment he showed you his true nature."

"Yes. Which is, I believe, the very reason that he is no better pleased to find me here than I am to find him. He can comfort himself with the notion that he was considered an innocent bystander, or even a victim, in this incident and that no one here will care what I have to say, regardless. But he cannot be truly easy in his mind knowing that I *know* the real measure of his character," Christopher said, and Arabella thought he looked grimly pleased at the thought of disturbing Sir Randall's comfort.

"I very nearly just said that I have kept you long enough with my tale, Lady Arabella, as I am speaking at a much greater length than I intended, but as I recall, *you* are the one keeping me. You are a most unexpected creature, you know. I should never have dreamed that I would find myself willingly pouring out this story to anyone."

"I fear I cannot bring myself to apologize, sir," Arabella smiled companionably at Lord Willingham, and wondered a little at how at ease she felt with him. Between his shocking tale and the fact that she was spending such a great length of time unchaperoned in the company of a scandalous gentleman, she really ought to have felt much more tense and anxious.

"I do not require an apology, which is odd considering the fact that I was decidedly anxious to be rid of your company as quickly as possible," he shrugged bemusedly and returned her smile. "But I will finish the story quickly nevertheless, before a search party is sent out for you."

"Thank you," she said.

"As I said, I was with my friend when he attempted to reason with Sir James, and when that conversation ended poorly, he told me that he was going to call the man out. It was well known that Sir James was proficient with pistols, and I persuaded my friend that he should find another way to make the man pay for his sins. After all, getting himself killed in a duel, would not help his sister.

"My friend decided to return to his quarters to write to some distant relatives for advice and assistance. I have cursed myself many times over for failing to stay at his side in a time of such trial, but I had business of my own to attend, and I left Town that same afternoon, charging him to contact me immediately if he required my help. I thought he had taken my advice, or would find some understanding with his relatives. I thought…" His voice trailed off, obviously reliving the agony of that moment.

"You did nothing wrong," Arabella said reaching for him instinctively, for the grief and self-loathing were palpable in Lord Willingham's voice. "I am sure very few friends would have done so much, really."

"It was not enough. From what details I managed to piece together later, my friend went out a few evenings later and overheard Sir Randall laughing to a group of his friends about the affair. It was simply more than my friend could bear, and he challenged Randall to a duel. Suffice it to say, Sir Randall was the winner in that matter, and my friend died, shot down in the street. When word of his death was brought to his sister, she appeared to take it rather calmly, I was told. And then she walked out of the front door of her aunt's house and with perfect deliberation flung herself into the sea."

Arabella gasped.

"I am sorry," he said belatedly. "I should not have shared the whole tale. It is too gruesome for a lady."

"No," Arabella said softly dabbing her lips with her handkerchief. "No. I asked. And it is important for me to know what sort of scoundrel I am dealing with."

"*We* are dealing with," Lord Willingham said softly.

CHAPTER 11

Arabella rode home in the soft golden light of early evening, but she could have sworn that it was as dark and cold as midnight. She could not rid herself of the lingering effects of Lord Willingham's story, nor indeed was she altogether certain that she ought to be rid of them. It would be very important, if she were to save Ellen from marrying such a monster as Sir James Randall, that she keep the facts clearly fixed in her mind of just what the man was capable.

For all his rough manners and plain speaking, Lord Willingham had seemed genuinely concerned for her when she bid him farewell.

"Never forget, even for a moment, that you are pitting yourself against someone without pity or remorse," he had cautioned her once he had gently assisted her back onto her horse. "He cares for absolutely nothing but his own self-interest, and if he feels you are a threat to his goals, he will do everything in his power to stop you, however best amuses him."

The truth of those words was all the more chilling, Arabella thought, because it was quite likely that Sir James already suspected that she distrusted him. She recalled the mocking way in which he had attempted to get her to admit she disapproved of his secret correspondence with Ellen, and his implications that she was cold-hearted and unfeeling.

She had done her best to appear neutral and supportive when speaking with Ellen since then, but reflecting back, she could see that Ellen must have felt her lack of enthusiasm. Indeed, it had been two days since Ellen had even spoken with her, and that in and of itself was highly unusual. If she had not been so preoccupied with cornering Lord Willingham into speaking with her, Arabella realized that she would have felt something was amiss.

Perhaps, Sir James was already subtly persuading Ellen to distance herself from Arabella, and that was the last thing Arabella would want. Rectifying that would mean —horribly—that she would have to pretend to be delighted with the engagement and enchanted with Sir James. Anything less would only serve to rouse Sir James' suspicion and push him to alienate Ellen from her altogether. Such blatant prevarication would be distasteful, to say nothing of difficult, but Arabella was determined not to play into Sir James' hand.

Having forced poor Lord Willingham to confide in her, she would take great care to put his experiences to use and not make the mistakes that others had made with Sir James.

Unbidden, an image of Lord Willingham appeared in Arabella's mind and she smiled. He had looked positively stricken when she rode up and insisted on speaking to him. The very idea of a great, strapping man with a reputation such as his being afraid of her was laughable, and yet there was no denying the hunted, wary look that had been on his face. Of course, the look in his eye was quite different when he had been adjusting her bonnet. She shivered with the thought and a delicious thrill went through her.

"Why, there you are," Marianne called, coming around a corner of the stable and startling Arabella. "No one knew just where you had taken yourself off to this afternoon."

"I fancied a ride," Arabella explained, rather unnecessarily as she allowed a groom to help her down from her horse. "It's a lovely day for it, after all."

"Well, it seems to have done you some good. You look happier than you have in days."

"Do I?" the observation struck Arabella as odd, considering the dark threat of which she was now fully aware.

"Yes, your smile just now as you rode up, at least. It looked as if you were thinking of something very pleasant," Marianne explained.

"Just the lovely weather, and how relaxing a little bit of solitude proved, I suppose," Arabella replied. Perhaps Marianne was simply making polite conversation—

although that would be decidedly uncharacteristic or perhaps, she was unskilled at reading expressions, Arabella thought idly as they walked arm in arm up to the house. She hadn't been thinking of anything even remotely pleasant.

"Are we still going over to the Millworths to play cards this evening, or are you too worn out from your long ride? You won't have much time to wash and change, and I thought you didn't seem particularly enthusiastic at the prospect of going when we discussed it this morning."

"Oh, no, let's still go," Arabella answered firmly. "I didn't mean to be so long, but I can be ready shortly. It would be too rude to cancel after accepting their invitation, and I haven't seen Ellen in two days running now. Besides, it is one of the few social activities that Father seems to actually enjoy taking part in, and yet you know he will not go unless we do. I would hate to deprive him." There was no time like the present, after all, to begin her charade of enthusiastic support of Ellen if not her despicable beau.

"That is true enough, and I think it will do Daphne some good to get out of the house and be around other folk for a time," Marianne agreed. "She has been so miserably out of sorts, and Mrs. Millhouse has always had a way of cheering her."

"I am to blame for Daphne's being out of sorts, I know," sighed Arabella even as she quickened her pace towards the house. "It is unforgivable, the way I've avoided dealing with her and left it all to you these past few days, Marianne."

"You very clearly have had something weighing on your mind," Marianne replied simply. "There is nothing unforgivable about being preoccupied on occasion. And as I told you before, it is not necessary for you to always be trying to make up for our lack of a mother."

"You are doubtless correct about that, yet I would not have intentionally chosen to withdraw from my usual role so suddenly and unexpectedly. It is disruptive, and rather unfair, I think. But there are... delicate matters, I suppose I may say, which I cannot put off until a more convenient time."

"You do not have to take me into your confidence, although I will tell you plainly that I wish you would. When have we ever had secrets from one another, Arabella?"

"Never, in my recollection," Arabella said. She could not recall ever keeping even the most trivial of concerns from Marianne, to say nothing of something so monumental as recent developments. It was unbearably tempting to tell her sister everything, which, indeed, was why she had done her best to keep to herself for the past few days. But her conversation with Lord Willingham still echoed in her ears, and Arabella knew that involving even someone whom she trusted implicitly was too great a risk. Sir Randall was simply too dangerous, and above all, she wanted to keep those she loved safe from the man.

"Until now," Marianne observed, correctly interpreting Arabella's prolonged silence.

"Yes, until now, I am afraid. Pray do not be angry with me, Marianne, for I would gladly tell you if I were able. Indeed, I *will* tell you all, the very instant that I can. But for now, I must beseech you to be patient with me a little longer."

"You certainly do not need to beseech me for anything of the sort," contradicted Marianne, with a reassuring smile that warmed Arabella's heart and soothed her overwrought nerves a great deal. "I know you will tell me as soon as it is possible, and I know furthermore that whatever you are so preoccupied with must be extremely important. Go on, make haste. Get dressed or we *will* be late."

"Is Letty back from her mother's?" Arabella asked.

"I do not believe so," Marianne said, "But I will find Dora and send her to you."

"Please" Arabella said and Marianne nodded her assent. The maid would have her ready posthaste. Ready for what, Arabella had yet to discern.

CHAPTER 12

"It's so good of you to come," Ellen greeted Arabella, but there was a distinctly chilly note of formality in her tone. The Ellen Millworth of a fortnight ago would have been unable to restrain herself from embracing Arabella and squealing with delight the moment she set foot out of the carriage.

"Of course, you know we wouldn't miss it for the world," Arabella replied brightly. "And I've been longing to speak with you. I cannot think of a time when we were both home that we went two whole days without seeing one another! It's unheard of."

"I have been quite occupied, of course, with making decisions and preparations for the wedding," said Ellen, more stiffly than ever. Arabella felt her heart break a little at the sudden distance between them, a distance which had never existed before in her memory, and which seemed unbearable. Still, she kept her smile in place determinedly.

"Why, naturally you wouldn't be able to think of anything else! I shouldn't wonder if you lie awake half the night thinking of it all, there are so many decisions to be made. But you must tell me every last detail that you *have* settled on, for I have been dying to hear all about it."

"Truly?" asked Ellen, looking both wary and hopeful.

"What on earth can you mean, truly?" asked Arabella forcing herself to laugh lightly. "You are my dearest friend in all the world, and you are to be married. Whatever else could possibly be occupying my mind at such as time as this?"

"Of course! Arabella. Only—" Ellen broke off and glanced around at the small group of guests scattered about the brightly lit drawing room. She met her fiancé's eyes and seemed to be experiencing some internal struggle. Sir James was caught in a jovial conversation with Ellen's father and several other gentlemen, and, unless Arabella was mistaken, he was not overly pleased at being unable to immediately interrupt her discussion with his intended victim.

"What is it?" asked Arabella, lowering her voice and moving subtly away from the rest of the guests so they might speak at least semi-privately, and taking care to stand so that she obstructed Sir James' view of Ellen. "Only what?"

"Only I had thought, it seemed that perhaps you did not care over-much for Sir James and did not approve of our match," answered Ellen in an even lower voice, eyes downcast.

"Even if that were true, would it mean that I cared any less for our friendship?" demanded Arabella, a little hotly. "We have been friends all of our lives, and I cannot imagine any difficulty which might keep us apart."

"You are right, of course. I know that I only thought you might want some... some distance, I suppose. You might not care to hear me chattering on endlessly about the menu for the wedding breakfast or my gown, or things like that, and I really cannot seem to think of anything else. Well, aside from thinking of how much I love Sir James, and you mightn't care to hear about that either."

"Dearest, of *course* I want to hear you chattering on about every last bit of it. I wouldn't miss a single word, not for a thousand pounds. I only want to see you happy, you must know that, and if Sir James is what makes you happy, then you must have him. Indeed, if he makes you happy then we will keep him hostage here if we must!"

Ellen laughed delightedly at Arabella's jest and did not seem to notice the slight emphasis that her friend placed on the word 'if'. Arabella hadn't meant for her to notice it, but the qualification was desperately important for her own peace of mind. Lying to her best friend was utterly distasteful, and she found that she couldn't quite stomach it.

"I believe he would be a very willing hostage if it came to that," Ellen replied, and her smile was genuine for the first time that evening. "Although Sir James has asked me if I have gotten my hands on some sort of love charm or potion, for he declares that he is entirely besotted by me."

"As if a girl with even a quarter of your charm and beauty would need any such thing as a love charm! Sir James must count himself the very happiest of men to have caught the notice of such a prize as yourself."

"Oh, Arabella, I am terribly relieved to find that you are happy for me after all," exclaimed Ellen, flinging her arms around her friend ecstatically. "I *told* Sir James-"

"Told him what, dearest?" prompted Arabella gently when Ellen broke off her speech suddenly.

"It was silly, that's all. He somehow got it into his head that you might harbor a dislike for him, or any other gentleman I could have fallen in love with as if I could fall in love with anyone in the entire world besides Sir James! But it sounds dreadful, of course, but he thought perhaps you might wish me to remain single as long as you yourself were unmarried. So that you might not feel the loss of my companionship. He could never imagine such a thing if he *knew* you," Ellen added hastily, seeing Arabella's expression darken at her words. "*I* did not think such a selfish thought had a place in your nature. But you *did* seem so displeased and aloof when you met him, and I began to wonder…"

"Ellen, I would walk through fire rather than cause you distress, knowingly or unconsciously," Arabella said firmly, thinking that she could cheerfully have murdered Sir James Randall for this alone. "I never dreamed that you would imagine I was thinking such a thing. Indeed, I can assure you that such an idea has never crossed my mind for even the slightest instant. If I seemed distant last evening, it was due to my struggles with Daphne earlier that day."

"Of course, that explains it," Ellen said, her entire countenance seeming to rest back into the bubbling joyfulness that was her natural state. "Has she been very dreadful?"

"Hideous," averred Arabella with great solemnity. "More so than usual, I am afraid. You do remember the blue silk with the silver thread embroidery?" she asked, thinking that sharing Daphne's fit of temper would more than cover her own neglect of her friend.

Ellen nodded. "It is so beautiful, and to have such a gown, even though she is not yet out…"

"Was," Arabella said. "It *was* beautiful. In a fit of temper, Daphne chucked it into the fire," Arabella said tartly.

"Oh, no!" Ellen covered her mouth with dismay and stared at Arabella wide eyed.

"Oh, yes. Poor Letty burned her hand trying to rescue it."

"I can't believe that Daphne would do such a thing."

"She just doesn't think before she acts," Arabella said. "It is my own fault for spoiling her so, and I have kept to myself these past few days because I find myself in the position of having to examine the ways I approach… everything, actually. I did not want to put a damper on your joy, but I see now that I was foolish to stay away, as it caused you to imagine much worse explanations for my distance."

"I have been terribly foolish, to even entertain such notions," Ellen returned apologetically. "I can't imagine what came over me, only I have been feeling so upended as if my entire being were suddenly rearranged into a new person altogether."

"I imagine that would take some getting used to," laughed Arabella.

"Telling secrets, ladies?" Sir James asked, coming up to them with a teasing expression on his handsome face. "I would beg to be taken into your confidences, for they appear most intriguing, and I am forever at the mercy of my curiosity."

"Why, we have that in common, then, Sir James," exclaimed Arabella, hoping that she could present a convincing semblance of delight. "I have been begging your fiancée to tell me every last detail about the plans for your wedding, for I am positively wild with curiosity."

"Are you, indeed?" he wondered, and Arabella knew that she was not imagining the look of evaluation that came into his eyes as he spoke. Lord Willingham had been correct, she saw, in saying that Sir James would see her as an opponent if she were not careful and indeed, the vile creature had evidently already attempted to alienate Ellen from her. He would not have bothered, Arabella thought, if he hadn't seen her as a threat to his plans. She knew she must disarm his suspicions of her, no matter how distasteful a task it might be.

"More than words can say," she answered lightly. "Indeed, as I was just telling Ellen how sorry I was for seeming so out of sorts at the soiree. I am afraid I was terribly preoccupied with some difficulties I have been having with my youngest sister."

"Arabella has all but raised her sisters, you know," Ellen chimed in. "She has always felt greatly responsible for their well-being."

"A great burden, I should imagine, for such a young woman," said Sir James, with every appearance of sympathy. Arabella found herself loathing the insincere kindness almost more than his hostility, but she smiled appreciatively.

"Yes, but certainly no excuse for poor manners. I do apologize if I made you feel unwelcome, Sir James. I assure you that I am utterly delighted at your engagement."

"Nothing could make me happier, for I know how Miss Millworth values your friendship. Her happiness is my first and only thought, you know."

"We are in perfect accord, then."

"Oh, and now I *am* perfectly happy," exclaimed Ellen, looking delightedly from Sir James' face to Arabella's and back again. "It is so wonderful to think of how much fun it will be once everyone is better acquainted, and we are all comfortable with one another!"

"Ah, but it may be rather dangerous, dearest," Arabella teased her friend, fighting to ignore the cold, sick feeling that ran through her veins. "Just think of all the stories I can tell Sir James here about the trouble we always got into as children! He may see you in an entirely new light."

"You are a treasure trove, Lady Arabella, for nothing would delight me more than to hear tales of my beloved in her youth," said Sir James, and Arabella was certain that she detected a challenge behind his gallantry. She had not yet convinced him that she was fooled by him, and she suspected that it would require a great deal of effort to lull him into complacency.

"Dear me, what a marvelous thing it must be to be so adored," she replied, fluttering her eyelashes and smiling insipidly at the wretched man.

Once the Sedgewick family had returned to Ashbury Place at the conclusion of the evening, Arabella felt that she might well collapse from exhaustion and mental strain. She had never felt so isolated in all of her life, she was certain, for no matter how trying things had been in the past she had always been able to confide in both Marianne and Ellen, and now she was cut off from everyone. Well, everyone except for Lord Willingham, she corrected herself mentally, bemused. That her only support came from a man she was forbidden from associating with was really the height of absurdity. If someone had told her a fortnight ago that this would be the case, she would have considered them insane. And yet, she found herself wishing she could speak with the man again already, to discuss the goings on at the Millford house. That wasn't *too* absurd, she decided. Analyzing the interactions of the evening with her sole ally would be both productive and helpful, surely.

It had been more difficult that she could have dreamed, keeping up her charade of friendly enthusiasm for Ellen's upcoming wedding. Each time she gushed about the joyous occasion, she just about cast up her accounts, but by the time she said her farewells she was hopeful that she had soothed Sir James' suspicions. He had remained persistently close, so that she and Ellen never had a chance of speaking privately again, but as the night wore on, he had stopped making quite so many wary glances at Arabella.

It would take a great deal of extended pretense to fully convince him, she feared, and just then she felt hideously tired. And yet, there was still one more responsibility that she had to attend to before she could take refuge in sleep.

Slipping into Daphne's bedchamber, Arabella had to hold back a smile at the sight of the obstinate girl very clearly pretend to be asleep as soon as she became aware of her older sister's presence.

"Dear me, if you are going to feign slumber like a little child, you really ought to try for a more relaxed expression," she said mildly, sitting down on the bed beside Daphne and smoothing her hand over the girl's unruly golden ringlets.

"I am not feigning slumber like a child," said Daphne crossly, turning her back to Arabella. "I am *attempting* to give you the hint that I do not wish to speak to you."

"Well, and that is fine, you need not speak to me if you do not wish it. But I must say a few things to you, and as you are not a little child and are therefore far too mature to put your fingers into your ears, I suppose you will have to hear me out."

"Then you had better say it at once and be done with it so I can get some rest," was Daphne's deliberately unencouraging response.

"I wanted to tell you that I am sorry for being cross and impatient with you the night of the soiree, but you must consider your actions. You are no longer a child. You will soon be a young woman. Actions have consequences."

From the frown between Daphne's eyebrows, Arabella was not sure she was getting through to her at all, but she continued. "I daresay you deserved a scolding, but you are not in the habit of receiving scoldings from me, any more than I am in the habit of giving them. I was very frightened that afternoon, and my fright made me realize some rather enormous mistakes I have been making. That isn't a nice feeling, to say the least, and I suppose I lost my temper as a consequence."

"Marianne said that you might say something like that," Daphne said, thawing enough to sit up and gaze levelly into Arabella's face. "It is silly to disagree with Marianne, as she is the cleverest person in our family, but I thought she must be wrong about this, at least. What mistakes can you possibly have made, Arabella?"

"For one thing, I have tried too hard to shield everyone. It *sounds* like a kind thing to do, I know, and my intentions were always good, but I have realized that it isn't fair to keep people from fighting all of their own battles. Perhaps Father would not find it so easy to be distant from us all if I had not wanted so desperately to keep him from being sad or bothered. And perhaps you would not find it so easy to act on your temper and impulses if I had not been so anxious to make you feel so loved at all times that I refused to ever let you be punished when you act in ways…unbecoming a lady. I have made excuses for you over little things, and I now fear that something larger might cause you more distress than I can shield you from. You are at the point in your life where a mistake might cause a lifetime of harm. Do you see what I mean?"

"I suppose I do," the girl replied slowly, her pretty brow knitting together in fierce concentration. "But I don't think anyone can blame you for trying to keep us all as happy as you could."

"You are sweetness itself to try and excuse me when you are still half furious with me," Arabella said, smiling and drawing her little sister close for a hug. "The blame would be well-deserved, however, for I believe that I have unintentionally sacrificed your long-term happiness, and that is inexcusable. What is worse, I fear, is that none of us know quite how else to behave than the way we have carried on for so long. Change is hard."

"So you think things may be rather unpleasant for a time, while we all attempt to sort everything out all over again?"

"Rather unpleasant may be a mild term for it, actually. And I daresay that I shall shock you by losing my temper more than once in the future. I may even shock you worse by staying out of matters entirely and letting Father deal with your misdoings."

"I expect Father will be a great deal more shocked by that than I will be," giggled Daphne. "I will try my very best to listen better, Arabella, and to think about consequences before I act. I do not believe you can blame yourself entirely for my impulsiveness, though. I suspect, I would be nearly as bad no matter who had the raising of me."

"That is an oddly encouraging way of looking at it," Arabella laughed. "Now I have kept you from your slumber long enough, and I am more than ready for my own bed. Thank you for listening to me, dearest."

"I didn't really have much say in the matter," Daphne pointed out tactlessly. "And I don't know if I can go to sleep *now*. I have so much to think about, besides being a little annoyed that Marianne was right after all."

"It is certainly provoking how often she is right, but we must love her in spite of that."

"I suppose so," agreed Daphne with a comical show of reluctance. "Goodnight, Arabella."

"Goodnight darling."

PART III

CHAPTER 13

Lady Arabella found herself pacing in her pale blue morning dress. Luckily, she had worn sturdy walking shoes rather than her slippers which would have already been ruined by the damp grass and the uneven ground beneath her feet.

It had taken some doing to find a way to arrange a discrete meeting with Lord Willingham, but she found that she rather relished the challenge. It, at least, was a definite, concrete task with a clear measure of success unlike her real challenge of thwarting Sir James Randall. In that area she felt as if it were impossible to make any progress whatsoever.

The abandoned stone dovecote that was slowly crumbling to ruins on the edge of the Ashbury estate was decidedly dusty and drafty, but as no one had any reason to venture there, they were unlikely to be discovered, and that was all that mattered.

"Whatever am I going to do?" Arabella groaned, more than a little surprised at the unladylike tone of her own voice. "I cannot possibly keep up this charade much longer. If Ellen weren't so utterly bewitched by that horrible creature she would surely have noticed long before now how false and insincere is my every word. I hate lying to her, but what else can I do?"

"I believe you have chosen the wisest course of action, Lady Arabella," Lord Willingham replied evenly.

She could not claim that either his voice or manner seemed particularly soothing, yet she felt oddly soothed by his presence, nevertheless.

"How wise can it be, when I have accomplished *nothing* in the length of an entire fortnight?" she demanded, whirling about impatiently. Dust motes, glinting in the shaft of sunlight that streamed through the single window high in the old stone wall, swirled about her in sympathy. She did not notice them, or the distinctly admiring gaze with which Lord Willingham regarded the sight. "Ellen will be wed to that monster before I have managed to so much as cast a shadow of doubt in her regard for him."

"If you had attempted a more direct approach, I assure you that Randall would have alienated Ellen from you so entirely that you would be unable to so much as speak to her. It must be unspeakably difficult to maintain this ruse, I can appreciate that, for there is nothing I would like half so much as to horsewhip the scoundrel. But unfortunately, there is really no other strategy that I can see which offers any hope of success. He is too entrenched in society, and more so, entrenched in your friend's heart. The best strategy is to open her eyes to his deception."

"I struggle to believe that this miserable strategy has a hope of succeeding," Arabella sighed, starting to sit down gingerly on a rickety bench that was none too clean, but changing her mind. The pale blue muslin of her gown would show every speck of dirt and it would be too difficult to explain how she had managed to ruin it. Instead, she began to pace. "He still does not entirely trust me; I can sense it. He is careful to never allow Ellen and I more than a few scant moments of private conversation at a time. He is always, always present, like some vulture overhead."

"Do not be entirely discouraged," Lord Willingham said, taking out a linen handkerchief and spreading it on the bench so that she might safely take a seat. "Sit down," he said solicitously, but she was wracked with nervous energy. Lord Willingham continued. "For one thing, I believe that you *have* allayed the majority of his suspicions—at this point, with such a great fortune as Miss Millworth's on the line, I imagine Randall is careful to keep watch over all of her conversations with anyone who might influence her, so it is not just you he distrusts. For another thing, the friend I have asked to act as my agent and inquire into Sir Randall's business in London has written to inform me that things are not altogether adding up."

"Why didn't you say so at once?" Arabella demanded, then rushed on without waiting for his answer. "And what does that even mean, things are not altogether adding up?"

"Do sit," he said arresting her nervous pacing. She glanced at the handkerchief on the bench. "Thank you, kind Sir," she said as she seated herself primly on the edge of the bench.

"Nothing of the sort. I just can't abide your nervous pacing," He replied.

"I see nothing wrong with him," she said. "At least nothing I can put my finger on. It is all no more than a feeling. However, shall I convince Ellen of the fool-hardiness of her attachment?"

"I do not think you shall do so," said Lord Willingham.

Arabella groaned and covered her face.

"Do not despair," he said. "Although his business affairs seem perfectly respectable and legitimate at first, and even second glance, they will not bear up to further scrutiny. I am sure of it." Lord Willingham was rather maddeningly calm and cryptic in his response.

"I daresay you know perfectly well that that doesn't tell me anything of substance," retorted Arabella shortly, sparing her companion an irritated glance and shifting on the improvised seat that he had offered to her. "Besides, the wedding date is fast approaching."

"There is a weakness, a flaw in his façade, and as such we can certainly attempt to exploit it and potentially reveal his true nature to the rest of the community," Lord Willingham persisted, frowning obstinately. "You must have patience, that is all, and allow my friend time to discover real, tangible evidence that Sir James Randall is not all that he appears."

"My patience is in increasingly short supply," admitted Arabella ruefully. "And your friend is inordinately slow."

He raised an eyebrow, and she relented enough to smile at her reluctant ally. "It becomes more and more likely every day that I shall lose my temper with Sir James and either announce my loathing and disapproval publicly or else do the world a great service and poison his afternoon tea."

"No magistrate in the world would convict you, I am certain, but try to keep that particular plan in reserve for the time being," Lord Willingham said, and the answering smile on his generally serious face was more heartening than it ought to have been.

Arabella could not help herself. She burst out laughing, although the whole ordeal was no laughing matter. "I suppose I am very silly and selfish, complaining to you of such relatively small annoyances when you have received much more grievous injuries from Sir James. But I cannot help feeling terribly isolated in all of this. I cannot unburden myself to either Ellen, or even to my sister for fear that she might accidentally alert Sir James to my intentions. If it were not for the fact that I can confide in you, Lord Willingham, I fear I might despair entirely."

"That, I believe, is a key aspect of Randall's talent. He has a way of making his victims feel utterly isolated, and once someone is alone in the world, then despair does indeed come easily."

Arabella winced slightly at that. "Oh dear, I have misspoken once more and reminded you of your own woes. I did not intend-"

"Pray do not trouble yourself for even the slightest instant, Lady Arabella."

"No, I have once again spoken selfishly, and I would ask for your pardon. I truly do appreciate everything that you are doing for my sake, and for Ellen's. You are under no obligation to assist me, I know, and doing so must be something of a strain."

"I fear my reputation as a scoundrel and cad must be far worse than I previously believed, if it is a surprise that I would work to keep a lady out of harm's way," Lord Haye's eyebrows quirked humorously at the statement, but Arabella was certain that she detected a trace of pain in his expression all the same.

"Your reputation is indeed a fearsome thing, sir," she replied, keeping her tone as light as she was able. "But I did not mean to imply that you are painted as such a complete ogre as that. Dear me, I cannot seem to manage to express myself adequately at all today. It will most likely be a relief to you that I must pretend to be a complete stranger when we meet at Lady Gatwick's ball this evening."

"Ah, yes, I was both surprised and impressed to have received an invitation to the festivities at Gatwick Hall. I can only imagine that Lord and Lady Gatwick will be equally surprised and far less impressed when they realize that I have accepted their hospitality. It *was* your doing, I suppose?"

"Oh, it was hardly a difficult feat to accomplish. I offered to help Lady Gatwick with some preparations the other day, and while I was talking with her, I merely made a few innocent observations that, I suppose, prompted her to include *all the* gentry. I am afraid that I am rather good at getting people to do things, in general, that they would not have thought to do if left to their own devices."

"I can personally attest to the truth of that statement," Lord Willingham laughed ruefully, gesturing around the dusty room. "As I distinctly recall vowing to never so much as speak to an eligible young lady in this town lest I be actually run out of my own home by an angry mob. And yet here I am, in what most people would consider to be a rather compromising situation with the most eligible young lady of them all."

"Oh I am not," protested Arabella quickly. "And that is most certainly, not what I meant." Blushing, she stood without fully meaning to do so. "Generally, I am so intent on keeping the peace and making certain that everything goes smoothly that I fear I have developed rather a knack for persuasion. It is exceedingly uncharacteristic of me to behave in this manner, and I certainly comprehend the risks involved. I apologize, again, for pressing you into this situation."

"And I will tell you again that your apology is not needed. *My* reputation is already an utter loss, as you well know. You are risking a great deal more than I, for if our collaboration is discovered it is your reputation that will be ruined."

"Oh," she breathed. She knew it was so, and yet had not ventured to put the risk into such uncompromising words.

"And then, you will have no recourse but to marry me, the impecunious and disgraced heir of a weak-willed wastrel," he said. There was jollity in his voice but a strange light in his eyes.

Arabella felt her face grow hot. Lord Willingham was joking. He could not have intended for his words to be taken seriously, or even in a comforting way, and yet they most decidedly had that effect on her. It was strange, certainly, that what was the worst-case scenario seemed far less dreadful than it should have been. In fact, it was almost welcome.

"We must have a care not to be discovered, then," Arabella managed, and she knew that her blush had deepened a great deal.

"Indeed, we must," he agreed, offering Arabella a gallant bow as she did her best to hide her confusion by sweeping out of the dingy dovecote and into the bright sunshine and her mood lifted to a lighter feeling than she had embraced since the start of this whole charade. Her heart was beating a strong tattoo as if he had actually proposed to her. Of course, he did not. He would not. They had no attachment of any sort, and anyway, he was a rake. She would not marry a rake. No, replied the snide voice of her conscience. She would only meet him in a deserted dovecote.

CHAPTER 14

If Arabella had hoped that Lord Willingham's presence at the ball at Gatwick Hall that evening might go mostly unobserved, those hopes were dashed within minutes of her own arrival. She stumbled haplessly into a knot of gossiping matrons almost at once, and they were more than delighted to forcibly include her in their outrage.

"I cannot believe that the man would dare to show his face among respectable people, not when he must know perfectly well that he isn't wanted," Mrs. Potterton, a perpetually scandalized woman of advancing years, scolded Arabella as furiously as if she suspected Arabella had invited Lord Willingham herself. Which, Arabella supposed, she had, in a way.

"The idea of a creature like that forcing his company upon decent people—I shouldn't wonder if Providence doesn't send a judgement upon him!" averred Mrs. Filmore, a scrawny and superfluous sort of woman whose sole purpose seemed to be that of ferreting out as many shocking stories as possible and creating them when none were present.

Arabella had known Mrs. Filmore since her own childhood and had done her best to be tolerant of the woman, who was a spinster of limited means, as it seemed rather pitifully obvious that being the first to spread a salacious rumor was her sole claim to importance. There was, however, a spitefulness to Mrs. Filmore, utterly lacking in her companion Mrs. Potterton, which had always kept Arabella on her guard.

"I was quite startled to see him, I can assure you," Lady Gatwick said, with enough genuine distress that Arabella felt a pang of guilt for maneuvering the poor woman into issuing the invitation. "I only sent the invitation as a matter of protocol—I never dreamed he would think of actually coming here. Why, he has been almost a perfect ghost about social affairs until very recently."

"Oh, I believe his sudden renewed fondness for social gatherings can be very easily explained—very easily explained indeed!" sniffed Mrs. Potterton, giving Arabella a significant glance. "I can hardly think it a coincidence that his timing aligns to perfectly with the return of our most eligible and sought-after young lady. After all, she was in Bath for most of the summer. You want to have a care, Lady Arabella," she added darkly. "Have a care."

"I assure you, Mrs. Potterton, I have no intention of associating with a gentleman of such tarnished repute.

You know me too well to think it for an instant, I should hope."

"I do, and I thank Providence that you have always had such a sensible head about such matters, I'll tell you plainly. But it never does to underestimate the power of a man like that. There's been many a girl every bit as sensible as you who has lost her head entirely to a man who looks less appealing than *that*."

"Indeed," Arabella murmured, and her gaze turned almost involuntarily to Lord Willingham, who was standing uncomfortably in a lonely corner, clearly attempting to avoid drawing attention to himself. She could feel her heart go out to him, and a sympathetic smile wanted to tug at her lips.

"Yes, indeed," sniffed Mrs. Potterton, and her glare turned so suspicious that Arabella came back to herself with a sharp jolt.

"I would forbear to speak of such things in the presence of an innocent young girl," began Mrs. Filmore, in a tone which indicated that she was all too happy to mention such things. "But-"

"Oh, I must beg your pardon, Mrs. Filmore, Mrs. Potterton," interrupted Arabella hastily, knowing that she would struggle to hide her anger if she were forced to listen to another false recitation of Lord Willingham's sins. She did not have time to wonder, just then, when she had become so certain that it *was* false, but she found herself entirely certain of it. "I promised my sister that I would ask Sir Hampton if he would lend her a book that she is desperate for, and I see him just over there. If I don't catch him before he makes his way to the billiards room, I shall never be able to capture his attention. Everything looks perfectly lovely tonight, Lady Gatwick."

Arabella hurried away with more haste than tact, leaving Mrs. Potterton sniffing disapprovingly in her wake.

Since Marianne really had asked her to see if Sir Hampton would let her borrow a book—he was a cross, elderly gentleman who had little use for most people, but possessed of a surprisingly soft spot when it came to Arabella and Marianne had insisted that he would not refuse *her* if she made the request—Arabella hastened to his side and engaged him in flattering small talk for a few minutes before venturing to mention the coveted volume.

"Hmph, and why doesn't your sister ask me herself if she's so wild to read the confounded thing?" he demanded, drawing together his truly impressive shaggy grey eyebrows forbiddingly.

"She's simply terrified of you, sir," replied Arabella archly. "Nearly everyone is, you know perfectly well, for you frighten them on purpose and do not deny it."

"But not you, eh? All the other little girls in the village have a tradition of being terrified of me, and yet I can't recall *you* ever being frightened of me, not beneath all your prim and proper ways. You have spirit under there, I always said. Puts me in mind of your mother, you know, back when she was a young slip of a girl."

"Do you really think I am like her?" Arabella felt a conflicting whirl of emotions at the elderly gentleman's observation.

"I certainly do. Grace and spirit, just laughing out at everyone behind good manners. Although I daresay you haven't been so inclined to laughing as she was. Why I recall my late wife saying, back before your mother married your father, that she didn't seem to take a single one of her suitors seriously. Hard to picture your father being laughed at, isn't it? It fairly drove him mad, especially when all the parish was certain that she would accept that wastrel Willingham."

"What?"

"Not to say that she took *him* seriously either, but most folks thought he would come out the winner, him being more dashing and exciting than her other suitors."

"Sir Hampton, whatever can you mean? Willingham? As in—"

"Yes, yes, old Lord Willingham, the uncle of that poor idiot over there, who was foolish enough to come here tonight even though he must have noticed no one wanted him about. Did you never hear that Willingham's uncle was once wildly in love with your mother?"

"That is…impossible," protested Arabella weakly, although she could see from Sir Hampton's expression that he was entirely earnest. "Isn't it?"

"Why on earth should such a thing be impossible, young lady? Your mother was a beautiful, vibrant creature, if it is not an impertinence for me to say so, and she fairly drew suitors to her as a flower draws bees. And there were no more bitter rivals for her affections than your father and John Hayes, the late Lord Willingham," he retorted decisively.

"But she chose Father."

"She did, and a wise choice it was, everyone hereabouts agreed. Willingham excepted, naturally. *He* was quite broken up about it. Sincerely, I believed. He left soon after and from all accounts proceeded to live his entire life thereafter as if attempting to either blot out her memory or prove her right that he was not worthy, I cannot say which."

"No wonder Father was so stern when he saw that Christopher, Lord Willingham, I mean, had come to stay here," Arabella murmured, and her gaze once more traveled to Lord Willingham's face without a conscious thought.

"Hmph. Everyone does say that young man is quite as wicked as his uncle before him, if not worse. Snubbed right and left ever since he arrived."

"Do *you* think he is wicked, Sir Hampton?" she asked impulsively, turning her eyes back to her companion's scowling, wrinkled face.

"Since you ask, young lady, I do not," he answered unexpectedly. "Although I daresay I shouldn't say such a thing to an eligible girl, should I?"

"Then why do you say it?"

"For one thing, I have yet to hear of a single thing the poor fool has actually done wrong. I mean verifiably, you know, not just rumors and suppositions. And for another thing," Sir Hampton paused and looked uncomfortable.

"What? Oh, do tell me, Sir Hampton," Arabella said coaxingly.

"Dash it all, it sounds foolish to say so, but he simply doesn't look the type to me. You *can* tell things about a person's character, I say, by the way they carry themselves or meet your gaze. Honest men look you in the eye, they do. The windows to the soul, and all that," he said. "You can tell things about a man when he looks you in the eye."

Arabella found she had to agree with him.

"Other fine young gentlemen I could mention, but there, that is simply supposition of a type as well. That is my opinion, and it is more than I imagined saying on the subject. Tell your pest of a sister that she may borrow the book if she is *exceedingly* careful with it, it is both rare and old. I shall have it sent over first thing if you promise to let me go to the billiards room in peace now."

"Of course, Sir Hampton, I am sorry to have kept you so long. And I am sure that Marianne will send her most sincere gratitude to you, but in the meantime, you have mine," Arabella curtseyed and smiled with such warmth and affection that she could see the tips of the old gentleman's ears turn a rosy pink as he harrumphed and stomped creakily away.

"Surely such a charming and beautiful lady can command a more gallant attendant," Sir James said, appearing suddenly at Arabella's elbow and watching Sir Hampton's footsteps with an expression of amusement.

She had to order herself to keep from scowling as she turned to greet the man. There was such a mean-spirited feeling to every word he spoke to her, nothing that she could ever reasonably pinpoint, but his antagonism was like an intangible slap, and she noted that he did not look at her, and when he did, he did not meet her eye. She was quite certain that Sir Hampton had been referring to Sir James when he had started to criticize 'other fine young gentlemen'.

"Sir Hampton's bark is much worse than his bite, I can attest," Arabella replied with a sweet smile. "People do tend to find him rather irascible, but he has always been very kind to me."

"The privilege of being a lovely young woman, I should imagine. He certainly has not extended any of that kindness elsewhere," Sir James sneered, and Arabella thought it was more than his usual affected mockery of everyone and everything. Sir Hampton must have slighted him somehow, or at least shown that he was not taken in by the oily charm that seemed to fool the rest of their community. She felt more affectionate towards the old gentleman than ever and could not resist the temptation to needle Sir James.

"I have always found Sir Hampton to be so terribly perceptive regarding the character and intentions of others," she murmured innocently. "Perhaps that is what makes him rather a terror to some parts of society. It is not entirely comfortable to have one's private opinions brought to the light of day, I suppose, but I always find a conversation with Sir Hampton to be wonderfully illuminating. He has a way of making an observation about myself that I would instinctively disagree with, and yet once I give the idea some consideration, I often find that it was perfectly accurate. Maddening, isn't it?"

"I suppose it would be, however, I have not had the privilege of having a cross old man read my character as if it were tea leaves," said Sir James, and Arabella was quite certain that he was both lying and unnerved. "I had thought to rescue you from the old tyrant, but as you do not seem to be in any distress, I shall return to my beloved."

Sir James turned sharply on his heels and crossed the room, taking out a handkerchief with a jerky motion as he walked. Arabella, watching his obvious irritation with no small amount of curiosity, noticed a slip of paper flutter to the floor in his wake. It must have fallen out when he retrieved his handkerchief, she realized, and decided immediately that she must examine it.

CHAPTER 15

Arabella soon discovered that retrieving the slip of paper would be something of a challenge. For one thing, she did not want to alert Sir James to the fact that he had dropped something. For another, it was not altogether seemly to bend down in the midst of a crowded room and pick something up off of the floor.

Making sure that Sir James' attention was fixed fully on Ellen, Arabella made her way as casually as she possibly could to the spot where the paper had fluttered to the ground. It was fortunate that it had come to rest near enough to a large oil painting. She could pretend to be admiring the portrait while she paused directly over the paper. She put her slippered foot on it, and paused looking around to see if anyone thought her movements strange. Walking slowly forward, her long, sweeping skirts brushed the slip of paper forwards along the smoothly polished marble floor and she was able to carefully make her way towards a low bench and there sit down to discretely retrieve it from beneath the hem of her dress. No one appeared to have noticed her sudden fascination with the painting, or her rather ungraceful movements towards her seat—or at least, Arabella hoped they hadn't. The small act of subterfuge was so nerve-wracking in and of itself that for a moment she forgot how anxious she was to discover what, if anything, the slip of paper contained.

"Probably nothing more than a note to his tailor, the wretched peacock," she murmured to herself as she unfolded and smoothed the uneven scrap. The paper was thin and cheap, nothing of import certainly. Her thought that she had risked making a fool of herself for nothing vanished as she realized that it was a torn fragment of a letter, one that had evidently been ripped into several pieces. She focused on the unfamiliar handwriting. The script was small and precise as if written by someone who was thrifty and would preserve the paper. It read:

"*…would caution you to proceed with all possible haste in your intended marriage if you are determined to stay this course of action. Sir Randall is not well known, but you might still be recognized and found out, Jame…*

She supposed the rip cut through the middle of the name, James? It did not tell her much more than she already knew. Disheartened, she turned the paper over and realized there was more writing.

She continued to read the small neat script even though the continuation of the message was not properly ordered and therefore was confusing at best.

"best chance to continue evading your sentence to the penal colony is to marry promptly and take your bride to live abroad..."

"What in Heaven's name are you doing?" Lord Willingham's sharp voice jolted Arabella out of her horrified trance. She could scarcely begin to take in the meaning of the words she had just read, but she realized that her expression must betray her distress.

"You can't be seen speaking to me," she said, looking up blankly at him.

"And you can't be seen sitting there as if you had just read your own death warrant," he answered impatiently. "Gather your wits at once before Randall notices that there is anything amiss with you. Whatever was on that paper you cannot risk letting him know that you read it."

"You are right, of course. I must speak with you at once, though. There is a small parlor upstairs that I know Lady Gatwick was not planning on opening up for her guests tonight."

"I shall meet you there in a quarter of an hour's time. In the meantime, you ought to dance with a few of your swains to avoid calling any further attention to yourself."

"Yes, certainly," Arabella ordered herself to not feel so stung by his words. The brusqueness of his tone did not bother her in the least—indeed, it had the effect of immediately bringing her to her senses, but she found herself resenting his casual mention of her 'swains'.

What an odd thing to mind at such a time! She found herself reflecting as he strode away from her side. She watched him leave, the powerful muscles of his back evident even through his jacket, or was that because she had seen him in his shirt sleeves, she wondered. A feeling of butterflies rolled up from her stomach and she realized that she didn't want to dance with any of her swains. She wanted to dance with him. That was an impossibility. He had not asked her, and even if he had, it would have incited gossip and ruined their chances at catching Randall out. Her heart was still racing, no doubt because she was nearly caught with the note in hand. If Randall had found her reading the note instead of Lord Willingham…No. She would not think such a thing. She would, as Lord Willingham suggested, find a dance partner and smile. That would mitigate any suspicions that Randall might have about her.

It was such a simple matter to catch the attention of a willing dance partner that she could hardly argue with Lord Willingham's assessment of the matter.

Arabella endured two dances with different young gentlemen, one of whom was actually on her list of eligible suitors to encourage. How strange to realize that she had not given that matter a single thought in weeks.

With new eyes Arabella studied Lord Albert Gresham, a sturdy, ruddy-cheeked gentleman of impeccable reputation, as he bowed to her at the completion of their dance. There was not a single thing she could think of that was objectionable about the man, she decided, and yet the idea of actually marrying him seemed entirely absurd.

"I suppose I cannot coax you to dance with me a second time this evening, Lady Arabella?" he asked politely, the admiration in his gaze clearly evident.

"Why, certainly not, Lord Albert!" she exclaimed laughingly, shaking her head in a teasing, flirtatious manner. "*Two* dances with the same gentleman would cause so much idle talk that I can scarcely contemplate it."

"A reputation as untarnished as your own certainly ought to withstand such a small misstep, but all the same I shall bow to your wishes now and ever," he replied, and the implication that she had only to utter a single word of encouragement was so heavy that for a moment Arabella could hardly think of any response that would not spur him on to make a declaration on the spot.

"Indeed, you are truly a kind friend," she murmured as blandly as possible.

"I shall strive always to be the truest and kindest friend that you might wish," he said, bowing once more and evidently accepting her dismissal for the moment, at least.

Arabella found it significantly more difficult to ease away from the dance floor than she had found it to procure dance partners. Indeed, she had to demurely decline no less than three invitations to dance, smiling warmly and claiming a slight headache, and a wish to visit the ladies' retiring room before she was able to fully escape the ballroom.

With a sigh of relief, she slipped down a deserted corridor and made her way, unobserved, to the upstairs parlor. It was a small room, and Arabella suspected that the less than fashionable furnishings were as much the real reason that Lady Gilbert kept it closed during parties as its small size and remote location. There was not even a fire lit in the hearth, she noted as she pulled open the door as quietly as she could.

Lord Willingham stood beside the cold hearth, restlessness written in every line of his body, a single candle resting on the mantlepiece, its light flickering appealingly over his features.

"I apologize for my lateness," Arabella said, a little breathlessly, closing the door behind her. "It was difficult to get away unobserved."

"My only concern is whether or not you are quite alright, Lady Arabella," Lord Willingham murmured, bowing slightly to her. "I daresay I have rarely seen anyone look so stricken as you appeared earlier, and I must admit that I did not care to see an expression of such abject horror on your face."

"That is far more kind than I deserve, I have no doubt," Arabella answered, rather taken aback at the genuine concern and sympathy that she detected in his face and voice. "I am a little better now, as I have been forced to compose myself. I will thank you for speaking to me as you did, and for intervening before I gave anything away. I confess that I lost my wits entirely for a moment, but I had experienced a horrible shock, as you will see."

Arabella removed the scrap of paper from her rose-colored sash where she had tucked it discretely before dancing.

"Sir Randall dropped this when he took out his handkerchief. I had needled him, I admit, and I think he was just shaken enough that he did not notice that the paper fell. Indeed, I doubt very much that he knew it was folded up among his handkerchief, for it would be a mad thing to intentionally carry about in such a manner."

Lord Willingham took the paper wordlessly from her outstretched hand, and Arabella felt her pulse leap unexpectedly when his fingertips brushed her own.

"This is... unbelievable," he said after a long pause, his eyes continuing to scan the few words repeatedly as if he could not believe what he saw written there. "As vile and wicked a scoundrel as I knew Sir Randall to be, I could never have guessed at such blatant calumny as this. I suppose I should not feel surprised at anything, for I already knew that he was capable of terrible deeds, and yet I feel shocked all the same. I don't wonder that you looked so stricken when you read this!"

"There can be no mistake, though, do you agree?" asked Arabella anxiously. "He is not who he said he is. I have been wondering this past quarter of an hour. Indeed, my mind has been racing so badly that it is a wonder I was able to remember the steps to even the simplest of dances! But is it possible that there is some other interpretation to this fragment? Might it be referring to someone other than Sir Randall? Or... I cannot think of any reasonable explanation."

"There can be no other explanation, I am certain of it," Lord Willingham answered, raising his eyes from the paper to Arabella's face. She could see something beyond mere anger smoldering in their depths and realized with a sudden jolt that before her was a man on the verge of violent action.

"I thought as much, myself, but as you said, it seems too fantastical to believe. *How* can a man, apparently sentenced for some crime and bound for the penal colony, pose so convincingly and successfully as a gentleman? Such a thing ought to be impossible!"

"I imagine it would be, for the vast majority of common criminals. But as I have said before, Randall—or whatever his real name may be—is a rare and particularly dangerous sort of man. Consider, with his brilliant gift of prevarication and his utter lack of moral scruples, coupled with his ability to charm nearly everyone into overlooking plain facts—why, it really ought to come as no surprise that he has been met with success thus far," replied Lord Willingham, in a voice that Arabella knew to be deceptively calm. Even in the dimly lit room she could see that his hands were unconsciously clenching into fists, as though he already had the fraudulent Sir James within his grasp.

"You are right, of course. I find myself amazed, beyond all the rest of it, at the sheer gall it must require to act upon such a scheme. If I had not seen Sir James appear rattled not half an hour ago, I would have supposed that he simply had no nerves whatsoever."

"Yes, you said you were needling him about something just before he dropped this—what had gone on between the two of you?"

"It was nothing, really," Arabella said, grateful that her companion was distracted from any wrathful action, at least for the time being. "I had been speaking to Sir Hampton, who I am really rather fond of, and Sir James approached me at the end of our conversation and made some offhanded sort of comment. I could tell that he didn't care for Sir Hampton, and actually, Sir Hampton had just alluded to the fact that *he* was not taken in by Sir James the way everyone else seems to be, so I revenged myself by speaking of what a perfect and unfailing judge of character I have always found Sir Hampton. It was nothing more than pettiness and spite on my part, and yet Sir James became visibly agitated."

"It is very telling, if you think of it carefully," Lord Willingham corrected her. "His greatest ally in this, or any other scheme is his ability to persuade those around him to see what he wants them to see and nothing else. Anyone who is less than entirely taken in is a threat to his very way of existence and therefore cannot be tolerated. I would not be at all surprised, if it were Randall's intention to remain in this neighborhood after his marriage, to find Sir Hampton dead within a month's time."

CHAPTER 16

Lady Arabella gasped wide-eyed. "Oh dear, I should not want to be the cause of such villainy."

"You are not," Lord Willingham asserted. "The villainy belongs solely to the blackguard in question."

"You think Sir James—I do not know what else I ought to call him—is really capable of *murder*? Of killing a frail old man?" gasped Arabella, even as she felt the accuracy of the statement.

"He is responsible for at least two deaths that I know of, one of which was carried out directly by his own hand, and I can assure you that he displayed not the barest instance of remorse," Lord Willingham reminded her.

"And now he is determined to marry poor, sweet, foolish Ellen," Arabella whispered, horrified afresh. "And by the evidence of this letter, he intends to take her out of the country, far from the reach of any friend who might help her. She is so close to her family. Her mother would be distraught. It is unthinkable, the kind of wretched existence she would lead—and if what you say is true, then he would have no qualms about ending *her* life once she ceased to be useful to him."

"He would murder her in her sleep without a moment of hesitation, but it will not come to that, madame. That I promise you." Lord Willingham swiftly placed the letter fragment in his waistcoat and strode across the room with such purpose that Arabella lost all remaining sense of propriety and clutched wildly at his arm.

"You must stop whatever mad idea is in your mind, I beseech you," she cried. "You cannot mean to confront him now—like this?"

"I will not allow him to pollute the air breathed by honest folk for even one instant more," snapped Lord Willingham furiously, but he did not shake off her grasp or attempt to push past her, at least. "Indeed, I ought to be horsewhipped myself for not attempting to expose him sooner."

"No, no indeed. I will not allow this," said Arabella with an attempt at infusing her voice with stern authority. She failed utterly there, but the result made Lord Willingham smile down at her in spite of his temper.

"You will not allow it, Lady Arabella?" he questioned; one brow arched humorously.

"Certainly, I will not. I have endured *weeks* of smiling in that insufferable creature's company, on your own advice, might I add. And it was sound advice, no matter how distasteful. Sir James is entirely too clever to risk a direct confrontation unless we have mountains of absolutely incontrovertible evidence, and you know that to be the truth, sir, even if you would rather-"

"Beat him within an inch of his worthless life?" Lord Willingham suggested with unnerving calm, but Arabella could feel much of the poised tension leave his arm beneath her grasp.

"Yes, well I feel the same, but as the weaker sex, we must be clever, rather than resorting to force, much as we might wish it. To be hasty will undo all the work we have done so far."

"I should infinitely prefer to beat him, but you are quite correct. Unfortunately, you are also correct in everything else you have just said. If you wish to throw in my face any of my earlier comments about keeping one's wits, I would certainly deserve it."

"I would rather we consider ourselves even, really," Arabella murmured, relieved at his willingness to listen to her. "Surely with the testimony of this letter your agent can discover Sir James' true identity in a short amount of time? And perhaps the fate of the *real* Sir James Randall as well. He must have come to some bad end, if—"

She broke off suddenly as the door opened behind her.

"Oh, I beg your pardon, I thought this room was not in use," came Mrs. Filmore's voice, making Arabella's blood run cold. She realized with horror that she—Lady Arabella Sedgewick—had just been discovered by the most inveterate, unforgiving gossip in the entire village in a position that even an innocent-minded person would find compromising. Alone in a dim, empty room, clutching the arm of a man who just happened to possess a reputation for being a terrible rake.

Mrs. Filmore could not conceal the sheer, malicious glee that she felt at such an unexpected windfall as she tittered unconvincingly, "Oh dear, dear, Lady Arabella, I would never have thought to find *you* in such a compromising situation, not with all of your insistence on constant propriety!"

"Mrs. Filmore," Arabella began faintly, with no clear idea of what she could possibly say. Fortunately, Lord Willingham intervened.

"Quite so, Mrs. Filmore. It is so unthinkable a scandal that I suspect that even if you attempt to ruin Lady Arabella by evil- minded gossip, very few people will believe you. In fact, I suspect that the more you attempt to convince people of what you have seen, the more likely everyone is to discredit the railings of a spiteful, idle woman."

"What on earth can you mean, you scoundrel? I have discovered the pair of you, as bold as you please, and have the proof of my own eyes!" shrilled Mrs. Filmore indignantly.

"Have you, though?" wondered Lord Willingham quizzically, and before Mrs. Filmore could splutter out a response, he had crossed the small parlor and vaulted lightly out of the open window, disappearing soundlessly into the night.

Mrs. Filmore let out a shriek—whether of alarm or anger, Arabella could not tell—and indeed, Arabella gasped in horror as well.

"The fool has killed himself!" Mrs. Filmore declared, rushing to the window as if anxious to see the bloodshed. Arabella joined her, feeling ill, but there was no trace of Lord Willingham on the hard paving stones two stories below, or indeed, anywhere else. It was as though he had grown wings and vanished without a sign. It was preposterous, and yet, Arabella realized however he managed to disappear, he had done so to save her reputation.

"We must have the grounds searched at once!" said Mrs. Filmore indignantly. Arabella rounded on her, attempting to think clearly through the overwhelming rush of relief that she felt.

"I believe that you will want to keep your tongue, Mrs. Filmore," she said coldly, drawing herself up with as much dignity as possible. "He was quite right, you know, there are very few people who will believe your tale in the first place. Who could credit the idea that *I* would be in such a ridiculously compromising situation with a man of such a scandalous reputation? And added to the fact that you have no evidence, you will appear doubly uncreditable once you claim that he leapt out of a window two floors up and made his escape unharmed. It is too incredible for words, you know. I shouldn't wonder if people might think your mind has been affected."

"How… how *dare* you?" gasped Mrs. Filmore, fairly quivering with outrage.

Arabella was not entirely confident that Lord Willingham's brash approach would be affective with the woman, and she was far from easy in her mind as to his actual fate—wherever had he gone? But she could see no alternative than to simply attempt to brazen the matter out.

"This situation strikes me as being exceedingly straightforward. As for how I dare, that hardly concerns you. All that you need to consider is whose reputation and standing in this community will fare best if you choose to attempt spreading rumors about me, madame."

"I…that is to say … I suppose I might have been a bit hasty, in ah, the manner in which I interpreted…" Mrs. Filmore stammered, losing a great deal of her righteous indignation as the truth of Arabella's words struck home within her heart.

"The manner in which you interpreted a perfectly harmless and innocent situation?"

"Ah, yes, that is certainly possible, in fact, it is the most likely explanation, I do suppose."

"Quite. I shall not keep you from enjoying the ball any longer, Mrs. Filmore," said Arabella as grandly as she could manage. She had never, in her entire life, spoken so haughtily to anyone, and she was convinced that the older woman would call her bluff at any moment.

"Yes, of course. Good evening, Lady Arabella," said Mrs. Filmore, stiffly withdrawing from the abandoned parlor, her cheeks aflame with indignant color.

Alone once more, Arabella allowed herself a moment to sag with relief. It was important she be seen dancing and socializing once more, and as quickly as possible, to thwart any suspicions Mrs. Filmore might raise if she changed her mind. But Arabella could not resist peering out the window, down into the gloom below where Lord Willingham had so mysteriously plunged.

Try as she might, she could make out no sign of the man anywhere, and she hastily abandoned the attempt and returned downstairs to dance as if she hadn't the slightest care in the world. It was the hardest thing she had ever done.

CHAPTER 17

The next afternoon Arabella occupied herself by poring over a worn edition of the peerage, examining the details of the *real* Sir James Randall's life and family. Doubtless the imposter had done the same and was unlikely to trip up over any such readily available details, but Arabella could not shake the idea that some key bit of information might be found. Besides, she was nearly wild with curiosity regarding Lord Willingham's daring escape of the previous evening, and she had to distract herself somehow or the other.

She wished she had thought to ask Lord Willingham for a copy of the fragmented letter, for in her distress and confusion the previous evening she could not be sure that she recalled the words perfectly. The author of the letter—and who *that* might be was maddeningly impossible to guess—seemed to feel confident that the real Sir Randall would not be easily missed or recognized. Why was that, Arabella mused, staring distractedly out of the solarium window. Was the man dead? And by some foul play?

A shower of fine gravel suddenly pelted the heavy leaded glass of the window, making her jolt in surprise. The rocks had been thrown, she realized, by Lord Willingham himself, standing at a safe distance from the house and nearly hidden in the deep shade of a willow tree. Her heart gave a quick, involuntary leap within her breast—from relief that he had not injured himself in the treacherous climb. She was certain it was only her worry for the man's well-being that filled her with tension.

Taking care to reassure herself that the solarium was truly empty, and she remained unobserved, Arabella waved her acknowledgement to him. She could just barely make out the slight smile that appeared on his face as he tilted his head peremptorily in the direction of the abandoned dovecote where they had met previously.

Nodding her agreement, Arabella rose immediately. Lord Willingham had vanished into the shadowy branches of the willow tree by the time she glanced out of the window a second time, whether out of general caution or a sense of haste, she could not tell, so she hurried out to the grounds without taking the time to collect so much as a bonnet or gloves, pausing only to pull on her walking boots so that her slippers would not be ruined.

She knew where they would meet: the abandoned dovecote. It was but a short walk. How had this become so commonplace, she wondered? Yet the excitement in her breast was anything but commonplace.

※

"You made excellent time, Lady Arabella," Lord Willingham remarked with some surprise when she rushed into the dovecote. "You must have practically flown across the grounds."

"Do not worry, I was not observed," Arabella answered rather breathlessly, smoothing her disordered hair. In truth, she was a little embarrassed at her unseemly haste, but curiosity and excitement had won out over decorum —a phenomenon which she feared was becoming a habit. "As for my flying, I assumed that was our new mode of travel, based upon your rather spectacular exit of last night. You are quite unharmed; I am glad to see."

"Ah, yes, I escaped entirely unscathed. I should almost be tempted to keep you in mystified amazement at my talents, but I must confess it was really a very straightforward egress."

"Indeed?"

"Yes. I had ample opportunity while I was waiting for you to notice that the parlor window was bordered by a fairly thick wisteria vine. I fancied that it might behoove me to observe any possible escape routes, just in case we were discovered. Fortunately, as it turned out. it was quite a simple matter to catch hold of the vine and use it make my way to the next window over," Lord Willingham explained in a matter-of-fact manner that Arabella found equally impressive and infuriating.

"That certainly explains why neither Mrs. Filmore nor myself were able to see any sign of you, or your shattered corpse, on the flagstones below," Arabella remarked, shaking her head in exasperation. "I was quite glad that we could not discover where you had gone, of course, but you cannot imagine how that mystery has been preying upon my mind in the meantime, and I never guessed at the actual solution."

"As it is hardly something that you would do yourself, Lady Arabella, you should not blame yourself for failing to guess what I had done," Lord Willingham said, the slight smile that she found so endearing playing on his mouth. "It is all but impossible to entertain ideas that are completely foreign to one's nature, I believe. It is why that wretch Randall, or whoever he may actually be, has such a distinct advantage over us."

"I would dearly love to agree with you, sir, but of late I have found myself doing a great many things that I would have said only a fortnight ago were foreign to my nature. The worst to date, I fear, was my treatment of Mrs. Filmore last night. She may be a petty and malicious gossip, but I would never have thought myself capable of speaking to anyone in such an arrogant and threatening manner."

"I overheard your conversation with her, as I was quite close by at the time," Lord Willingham said comically. "Do not reproach yourself, I implore you, for the manner in which you dealt with that foolish woman. Anyone as small-minded as she can only benefit from an occasional reminder of their real lack of importance and authority."

"I suppose so," conceded Arabella doubtfully. She moved more into the shelter of the dovecote, as an autumn wind had appeared, putting a chill in the sunny air. Perhaps, that was what gave her a shiver or perhaps it was thinking of Mrs. Fillmore and her own actions. Small-minded Mrs. Filmore might unquestionably be, but she was also fairly well known for her inability to forgive a grievance. The thought brought a spate of worry. She shoved it away. They had more important worries. "But have you found out any new information regarding Sir James?" She asked.

"In a manner of speaking, which is why I risked attempting such a bold meeting with you today. I had considered riding for London myself to carry our newfound evidence to my agent there, for I believe it to be quite an urgent matter, but I have instead decided to send it with an express courier. I fear what actions Randall might take if he begins to fear exposure, and I dare not leave the neighborhood for even the briefest of journeys, just as a matter of caution."

"I believe that is prudent, but what are we to do in the meantime?" Arabella wondered. "I have been examining the peerage until my eyes fairly ache, but I cannot find anything that might indicate the fate of the real Sir James Randall, or any other information of use, either."

"Do you feel that you have sufficiently persuaded Randall that you are no threat to his goals?"

"Perhaps." Arabella fixed him with her gaze. "Are you worried about my well-being?" she asked.

"I must say I am," he said.

His dark blue eyes were like a caress upon her skin, and she subconsciously brushed back the hair that had escaped her chignon. She should have worn her bonnet, and perhaps her pelisse. Nonetheless, a warm feeling of protection flowed through her. How could her father not see the goodness in this man, she wondered as she spoke?. "I cannot say with any real certainty that he is fooled, although I declare I have done all that was humanly possible to allay his initial suspicion of me."

"It will have to be enough, I think, for time is growing short," Lord Willingham said decisively. "Assuming that the letter was from someone whose counsel Randall will heed, and I think it must be so, for he evidently trusts that person enough that they have knowledge of his real identity and his current plans, then he will attempt to hasten his marriage to Miss Millhouse and we simply cannot allow that to take place.

"I think you must be right, but what would you have me do? I don't know how to stop it. Helen seems completely besotted. Lord save me from ever losing my head so over a gentleman," she blurted.

Belatedly, she realized that Lord Willingham was looking at her with a quizzical expression, his blue eyes dark with emotion. "You seem to be a woman much more in control of your sensibilities," he said softly. "A man would be a fool to try to trick you into an engagement. My thoughts are—" He broke off.

"What are your thoughts," she asked softly.

"I think, you would be much more of an aficionado to honesty, which is why this charade is such an anathema to you."

"Yes," she breathed, agreeing with him and yet wondering why his simple statement of fact seemed to bring a heat to her cheeks. He was only proving once again that he was a student of human nature. He seemed to know her more than she knew herself.

He cleared his throat, and paced away. "Two strategies have occurred to me," he said. "And I believe that both may be employed at the same time and complement one another. Or else I am entirely wrong, but it does seem that inaction no longer serves our ends."

"I agree, and I feel that I am willing -nay, even eager, to try any strategy that does not involve simpering in the face of that monster," said Arabella fervently. To her chagrin, Lord Willingham winced at those words as he turned back to her.

"Then you will be disinclined to favor half of my suggestions, I fear," he told her sympathetically.

"I should have known as much," she sighed. "Very well, what would you have me do?"

"I believe that you may be able to get Randall to let slip some minor discrepancies if he is sufficiently at ease with you. If, for instance, you pretend that in your vast enthusiasm for Miss Millhouse's impending nuptials you wish to put together a sort of... I do not know precisely, a collection of some kind that features anecdotes from both Miss Millhouse's childhood and Randall's."

"Oh, a kind of keepsake folio, that *is* a clever idea. I could say that I want to make a series of parallel illustrations or something of that sort. Ellen adores my sketches, so it would be simplicity itself to work up her enthusiasm for the project, and then Sir James could hardly refuse to cooperate," Arabella warmed to the idea despite its reliance on her continued pretense.

"Yes, exactly that sort of thing. I am hardly familiar with such ladylike occupations, but I had a vague notion, at least. It may come to nothing, I will admit, but then you never know when even the slightest detail may prove instrumental in bringing about the downfall of our common enemy," Lord Willingham said with enthusiasm.

"That is true enough," agreed Arabella. "But I hope that your other idea involves a little more direct action."

"A very little, I daresay, but it is worth the attempt, nevertheless. The elderly gentleman you were speaking to at the ball last night, the one who seemed to discomfit Randall, how much do you trust him?"

"Sir Hampton?" Arabella asked, nonplussed. Whatever she had expected Lord Willingham to say, it had not been that. "I trust him a great deal, as it happens. For all that I wanted to needle Sir James, what I said was perfectly true. Sir Hampton *is* a wonderfully reliable judge of character, perhaps because he has so little regard for sparing people's feelings as a general rule. He does not think that *you* are the dissolute rake that people say you are, I might add."

"He doesn't?" It was Lord Willingham's turn to be taken aback. "Why on earth not?"

"Dear me, the oddest and most unexpected things disturb your composure, Lord Willingham," laughed Arabella in spite of herself. "Fairly leaping out of a window into the night does not cause you to so much as bat an eyelash as far as I can tell, and yet hearing that a man does not believe you to be a great scoundrel leaves you agog!"

"Fortunately, Lady Arabella, you do not know what it is to be regarded with almost perfect universal scorn," Lord Willingham replied with some dignity. "It is my dearest wish that you never experience such a sensation, but I can assure you that it works quite strongly on the mind. I have been the heir of a terrible reputation for less than one year, and I became resigned to my lot in half that time. It proved to be utterly pointless to rail against my fate or attempt to change it, so yes, I daresay that I *am* taken aback at the novelty of finally hearing one person has a differing viewpoint on my character."

"One, forsooth!" she protested with exaggerated indignity, regretting her teasing words as she saw the genuine pain in her companion's expression. "Does my opinion count for nothing, then?"

"Your opinion, madame? I have been under the impression that you hold your opinion of me as immaterial, as I am your only ally in your quest to save your friend," he said stiffly, yet with the same straightforward directness that she always found so refreshing.

"Perhaps that was my reasoning, at first," Arabella admitted, speaking slowly. "But surely you must know that I have long since ceased to believe anything wicked of you, Lord Willingham. Indeed, I was delighted to hear Sir Hampton echoing my own thoughts on the matter. He said something to the effect that you simply do not *seem* capable of any real villainy."

"You both flatter me, then," he bowed, still rather formal, but Arabella noticed his stiffness and reserve lessen significantly. "But more to the point, Sir Hampton has a very high opinion of you, from what I observed?"

"I suppose he does. My sister Marianne has always declared that he has a soft spot for me. Indeed, that was why I was speaking to him at the ball. He has a famous collection of rare volumes and manuscripts, and she found out that he has in his possession something that she has been longing to read for ages, but she pressed me to ask him because he is more likely to say yes to me."

"Excellent. I wonder, if you asked him, in confidence, mind you—to apply whatever amount of pressure and suspicion onto Randall as he were able, would he agree to that request as well?"

"He just might. He does have some affection for me, and from what I gathered last night he does not care for Sir James in the slightest. He really is quite a perceptive old gentleman."

"It is something of a shot in the dark, I suppose. But my idea is that if we can focus his defenses on another person entirely, it may possibly distract Randall enough to make him let something slip when speaking with you," Lord Willingham explained.

"But might that not place Sir Hampton in danger? You did say last night that if Sir James chose to stay in this neighborhood for any length of time that you would be unsurprised to find Sir Hampton dead at his hand."

"It very well might, and I believe that if you decided to speak to him, you must attempt to fully impress upon him the potential danger, as well as the magnitude of Randall's wickedness. I would not ask you to place your friend blindly in harm's way, of course, but he is a man of some means, I believe. If he chooses to come to your assistance, he is well able to take measures to increase the protections around himself and his home."

"That is true. I believe I will speak to him," Arabella decided. "For all I know he will laugh me out of his presence, but perhaps he will listen. I had better go, now, before I am missed. I was in such a hurry that I did not even think of a reasonable pretext for my coming here."

"And we have tarried longer than I intended, yet again. That does seem to happen rather routinely when I speak with you, Lady Arabella."

"If you are implying that I speak too much, I suppose I cannot contradict you, sir," she retorted, nettled.

"I was implying nothing of the sort, I assure you. If you must interpret my words as having a deeper underlying meaning, you might take it that I am implying that time stops when I am with you," Lord Willingham said, and caused Arabella's heart to flutter yet again.

For one vast and eternal moment, she noticed everything about him: the scent of his cologne, the blue intensity of his eyes, the way his wavy hair fell across his forehead, the muscles always hidden under his jacket, except for that first viewing. Her lips parted, but she had nothing to say.

Without allowing her any further time to respond to his enigmatic statement, he bowed once and then strode out of the dovecote, leaving her to stare after him in confusion.

CHAPTER 18

Any number of gentlemen had said such complimentary things to her, and had made it clear that they *were* compliments, and yet she had remained utterly unmoved, Arabella reflected, baffled. Lord Willingham made his observation in such a casual way that it might have been nothing more than a statement of fact, and yet it made her blush speechlessly. Her hands felt damp and her heart raced. It was too provoking, she decided, and besides, the air in the dovecote was stifling in spite of the coolness of the autumn breeze.

She hurried outside without waiting a cautious interval after Lord Willingham's departure and could only curse her reckless haste and pray that Lord Willingham had been unobserved, when Daphne appeared at her side before she had made her way halfway back to the house.

"Whatever were you doing in the old dovecote?" demanded the child curiously, but without any trace of suspicion. She had evidently *not* seen Lord Willingham leaving, fortunately. "It's practically falling down, isn't it?"

"Indeed, it is. That is why I have always cautioned you to keep from playing in there," Arabella replied, concocting an explanation on the spot as convincingly as she could manage. "But it occurred to me today that we really ought not leave the poor old building in disrepair and neglect forever, and I wanted to examine it myself."

"Could it be repaired, do you think? We might keep doves in it once more! Were there ever any doves in it that you can recall? It has always been empty in my own memory," Daphne chattered excitedly, struck by the idea.

"Yes, I believe it can be repaired, but I do not know if we ought to use it for doves. Mother was terribly fond of them, you see, and I have always thought that Father ordered the staff to discontinue keeping the creatures because their noises reminded him too much of her," cautioned Arabella, not wanting the girl to become too attached to the idea, which she certainly would not have suggested if she could have thought of a better excuse for being there. "But there are any number of other purposes we could find for such a structure, aren't there?"

"I suppose so." Daphne sounded crestfallen. "But *I* love doves, and their cooing, especially. And no one ever told me that Mother loved them. It's something I have in common with her, and I never even knew it until this moment. It is too bad that all the things that might make me feel even a tiny bit close to her are too painful for Father to have around."

"Oh, Daphne, I am sorry. I have done a sad job of keeping her memory alive for you, haven't I?" sighed Arabella, stricken with regret.

"Yes, you rather have," Daphne answered frankly, but she slipped her arm around Arabella's waist in a friendly, forgiving manner to take the sting out of her words. "But you could always make it up to me, you know."

"And how do you propose I do that?"

"I propose that, for one thing, you try very hard to convince Father to let us keep doves here once more, because I really do adore them."

"I'll do my best," Arabella promised solemnly, hoping that her powers of persuasion would manage to extend that far. "What's the rest of it?"

"That you tell me at least *one* story about Mother every… week. I was going to say every day, but that might make you too sad. Once a week isn't too much to ask, I don't think. You could have the whole rest of the week to cheer back up again, and you know, eventually you might stop being sad when you think of her. I have been considering this, and I believe it's all a matter of practice."

"Perhaps, you may be right," Arabella said thoughtfully. "And you certainly ought to know more about Mother, there's no question about that. I hope you can forgive me for floundering so much and making such foolish choices, Daphne. I really have no idea what I am doing, you know."

"Oh, I do know, and I do forgive you, too. You really ought to go in and change now, though, Arabella. If *I* got my hem so filthy as yours is right now, I would get a frightful scolding."

ARABELLA WAS SO DRAWN IN BY THE REFRESHING APPEAL of speaking frankly with someone about Sir Randall's villainy that she could not forbear to wait long before meeting with Sir Hampton. Fortunately, the man had been as good as his word, and had promptly sent over the book that Marianne coveted along with lengthy instructions for the proper care and handling of such a rare volume, thus providing Arabella with at least a flimsy pretext for calling upon him.

She wheedled a basket of the delicate *chouquette* pastries that she knew were his particular weakness from the cook at Ashbury Place, and set a determined pace towards his nearby home.

"Here now, what's this?" the elderly gentleman demanded by way of greeting when she was announced in his bounteous library. Marianne, she knew, would have been unable to carry out a conversation in the distracting presence of so many fascinating books. Arabella was not half the student that her younger sister was, yet still felt the pull of the volumes herself. The scent of them was intoxicating and she would have liked to settle in to explore, but she could contain herself as Marianne, surely would not. She smiled thinking of her sister and her simple enjoyments.

"It is a pleasure to see you, Sir Hampton," Arabella said equitably, smiling brightly into the old man's scowling face.

"Oh! A pleasure, to be sure!" he scoffed, but it was really more from force of habit that he scowled rather than any genuine irritation at her presence, Arabella was certain. "And here I thought that by sending that book over to your sister right away I might buy myself a *few* days peace from your family. More fool I. I suppose. Now you'll be telling me that it didn't arrive, or it wasn't the right book, or it's been destroyed by that demon in child form you like to call Daphne Sedgewick."

"None of those things, sir. I came to call on you so I might deliver Marianne's note of thanks personally, along with a basket of our cook's *chouquettes*. You know you've always said that Hastings is the only cook this side of the Channel who can make them properly."

"Hmph. I may have said some such thing, in a moment of weakness. When *I* was a boy, we had a cook straight from a Parisian patisserie and *she* made them to a turn, I may tell you! No one else seems to manage it, but they do take one back."

He deigned to accept the basket, and lifting the cover, withdrew a *chouquette,* and took a generous bite, his eyes lighting with pleasure.

As he swallowed the morsel, he called to his staff to make tea and directed Arabella to the morning room.

"Now then," he said as they sat at the table and he dove into a second pastry, "my compliments to your Hastings. So. Now that you've sufficiently softened me up with delicacies, you may as well commence with telling me your actual purpose in coming to call today."

"You *are* terribly perceptive, Sir Hampton," Arabella laughed, shaking her head at both his poor manners and her own transparency. "And that is precisely why I wished to speak with you so particularly. But do not think too poorly of me for manufacturing an excuse, pray. For one thing Marianne *is* excessively grateful to you for loaning her that book, and I wanted to be sure we communicated our gratitude right away. For another thing, it is vitally important that my visit does not raise any suspicions, and this is a logical and convenient explanation for my coming here."

"Raise suspicions, is it? Merciful Heavens, girl, what are you going on about? You don't think you need a chaperone to pay a call on *me,* do you? Not that I'm not a fine and dashing specimen of a man, to be sure, but I can't believe that the gossip-mongers in this town have gone quite so far as to speculate on *that*? I won't credit it for an instant." Sir Hampton managed to look both outraged and mildly flattered at the same instant, causing Arabella to giggle undiplomatically.

"That is, I mean to say, no," she recovered, coughing delicately. "I have not heard any such speculations, although it would hardly surprise me, the idle gossips hereabouts being what they are. No, I must confide in you a rather lengthy tale if I am to explain my rather shocking statement, if you will indulge me, sir?"

"Proceed, by all means," Sir Hampton declared, taking another *chouquette* and settling back into his chair with an air of great interest. "My time is not so valuable as perhaps I make it out to be, and although my solitude is precious to me, I suspect that whatever recitation you have to make will be well worth the exchange."

"Thank you, Sir Hampton I am taking a risk, confiding in you, but I have always trusted your judgment, and you made a statement at Lady Gatwick's ball the other night that made me think you might be sympathetic to my perspective."

"Fallen in love with that disgraced wretch of a Lord Willingham, then, have you, child?" he asked complacently around a mouthful of *chouquettes*.

"What? No, not in the least," protested Arabella, staring at her companion in shock. She could not quite credit it. She wasn't in love with Lord Willingham, even though the very thought of him made her heart beat fast and her palms grow damp. She found herself looking forward to the time when they would next be together even if it was only to discuss that villain, Randall. She could not imagine what would happen when this escapade was over and she would no longer have reason to meet him in deserted dovecotes or empty rooms. The thought made her despondent. She would not think on it. "No," she sputtered. "I am not in love with anyone, indeed. This whole affair does not even truly, directly, at least, concern me. I have great misgivings about the man calling himself Sir James Randall, whom you know has recently become engaged to my dearest friend Miss Millhouse."

"*Calling* himself Sir James Randall?" Sir Hampton leaned forward, pastry crumbs dropping unheeded onto his worn waistcoat. "We shall set my first assumption aside for now, I say. Do not think for a moment that I shall be permanently distracted, but you had better explain yourself right now when you say the man is *calling* himself Sir James Randall. I'll grant you there is something distinctly sinister about the man, but why shouldn't he be who he says he is?"

"I know it sounds fantastical, sir, but hear me out, I beg you. If once I have explained my reasoning, you think I am only being foolishly suspicious, then I hope you will at least forbear mentioning what I say?"

"Oh certainly, certainly. I am practically a vault compared to every other member of this vociferous community." He pantomimed locking his lips with a key. "Well, out with it then," he said.

Arabella told him, as concisely and rationally as she could manage, a detailed recounting of her recent trials. The old gentleman listened attentively, making few interruptions and asking for clarification several times. When she concluded her tale, Arabella had to fight the urge to sag into her chair, so great was her relief at having an impartial listener. She only just realized what a burden she was holding in keeping this a secret.

"Well. Hmph. I might have lived a hundred years more and not predicted that *you*, prim and proper little Lady Arabella Sedgewick, would march into my home and tell me such a thing," he finally said after ruminating in silence for a few moments.

"Sir Hampton, do you mean that you do not believe me?" she asked, her heart sinking.

CHAPTER 19

"I mean nothing of the sort, child. Did I *say* I don't believe you?" Sir Hampton demanded irritably, scowling at Arabella. "Very well then. What I meant was precisely what I did say. I would never have expected this of you. I have done you a disservice, then, for not recognizing your courage and loyalty, and for not seeing that those qualities are at the back of your prim and proper behavior all along. You are more like your mother than I realized, and I already thought you were remarkably like her in some ways."

"But what of Sir Randall?" asked Arabella stubbornly. Sir Hampton tendency to examine one's character were all well and good, she thought, but she felt he was failing to recognize the most urgent priority just then.

"What of him? As you say, he *isn't* Sir Randall, and is apparently a sort of escaped convict. Your Lord Willingham—no, don't look so exasperated, I will say what I think, you know—*your* Lord Willingham, I say, has directed his agent to uncover the truth and we must hope for Miss Millworth's sake that the agent acts with the greatest of both alacrity and good fortune. There is precious little else that I can think of that anyone can do in the meantime."

"That is the other reason I wanted to speak to you so particularly," Arabella explained earnestly. "You see, it isn't any good *my* voicing suspicions and doubts as to Sir Randall's character, to say nothing of his identity! He is hard at work to make sure that we are rarely able to speak in private, and if he once more suspects that I dislike him then it is certain that he will do everything in his power to alienate Ellen from me. I am too close, you see. But *you* are barely acquainted with Ellen. As you said the other night, most of the inhabitants of this village are at least a little intimidated by you, and Ellen has been no exception to that."

"*That* is certainly true enough!" Sir Hampton chuckled, a little unkindly. "Miss Millhouse has been in the habit of looking askance at me since she was old enough to walk. But go on, I say. Doubtless you have a point somewhere in all of this."

"My point is that if someone who is not in Ellen's close circle were to start questioning Sir Randall's worthiness, he would not be able to isolate her from that person in quite his usual method, but those questions might give her parents enough concern that they would resist the hasty wedding that we fear he is going to attempt."

"Hastier than this already ridiculously brief courtship, I suppose you mean?"

"Yes, Lord Willingham and I both fear that if he heeds the counsel of that letter, he may attempt to convince Ellen to wed him within a matter of days. We need *something* to help us gain time until Lord Willingham's agent can uncover real, solid proof. And then, too, Lord Willingham thinks that if Sir Randall is dealing with an attack from another quarter, he may be more likely to let slip some detail in my presence."

"I suppose that is not an *entirely* foolish notion. You wish for me to make some less than discrete inquiries, ask some rather pointed and awkward questions, that sort of thing, is that it?"

"That was our general idea, I believe," Arabella agreed, trying her best not to wince at the man's cynical expression. "But I must disclose to you, sir, that if you agree to do so you will be placing yourself in what we fear will be very real danger."

"Danger? From what quarter?" scoffed Sir Hampton incredulously.

"Why, from the false Sir Randall, of course. Sir Hampton, from all evidence he is a desperately wicked scoundrel and will stop at nothing to accomplish his ends. I really must impress upon you that it is not any small risk to draw his attention to yourself as an adversary."

"The day has yet to dawn, my dear, that I waste even one solitary instant in fearing an insolent whelp such as James whomever he may be," Sir Hampton snorted, then waved a gnarled hand dismissively in Arabella's direction before she could fully articulate her protest. "Yes, yes, you believe he has killed before and will not be overly squeamish if it comes to killing again. You needn't become agitated on my behalf, young lady. I don't mean to imply that I won't take precautions to ensure my safety, but I *do* mean to imply that such a thing is not a consideration that will stay my hand. Nor should such a thing stay any true gentleman's hand in the defense of a lady."

"Thank you," Arabella said, a little wearily. "I hate to bring you into this, Sir Hampton, but there is truly no one else I feel I might ask for help. My own father is so prejudiced against Lord Willingham that I cannot imagine he would entertain a single word of this tale once he discovered that gentleman's involvement."

"I daresay you have the right of it there, my dear. But you may put your mind at ease, for I do not believe that I mind secretly playing the role of knight- errant for a change. Ordinarily, I only terrorize people out of boredom and irritation, you know. It will be quite refreshing to work towards a nobler cause."

"He is very devious, sir. You must not forget that even for a moment. Really, I am quite frightened of the man even when he is at ease. I cannot bear to think of how terrible he could be when he feels truly threatened," Arabella cautioned, feeling that her old friend was taking the whole thing with an attitude that was entirely too cavalier.

"Well really now, what can he actually do? Shoot me down in the street like a stray mongrel? Challenge me to a duel of broadswords? This is a civilized place, Lady Arabella, and even the worst of us are not in the habit of cutting down every aggravating person in the neighborhood. Fortunately for most," Sir Hampton wheezed out a laugh at his own observation.

"But you forget, Sir James is already convicted of at least one crime which was heinous enough for a judge to deem him unfit for civilized places," she said stubbornly. "At least, we can deduce that is true from the pilfered note. You must promise me that you will remain vigilant until this whole affair has concluded. Take all manner of precautions." She reached across the table and laid a careful hand on his skinny old arm. "Whatever would we do without you to terrorize everyone, after all?"

"There's a consideration, I suppose. Very well, my dear, I shall not laugh at your concerns any longer," the elderly gentleman conceded, and Arabella could only hope that he was in earnest.

○○○

Whether Sir Hampton really had taken Arabella's warnings to heart, she could not say with any certainty, but he had without a doubt embarked upon his mission with all possible haste. The very next morning she went to call on Ellen with a selection of lace patterns providing her with an excuse and Arabella found her friend in very obvious distress.

"Dearest, you haven't been crying?" Arabella exclaimed, taking in Ellen's tear-stained complexion and red-rimmed eyes. "Whatever can be the matter?"

"It is nothing, I'm sure," Ellen shook her head and sniffled heroically. "Only some silly talk, it doesn't matter in the least."

"People hereabouts *do* love their silly talk," said Arabella soothingly, drawing Ellen to a velvet covered settee. "But it is inexcusable for anyone to be upsetting you so badly. What on earth has been said?"

"Oh, I don't even know precisely. Someone has been asking very impertinent questions, and it has caused poor Sir James a great deal of distress. He has a very sensitive nature, you know; it comes on account of his poetic, passionate spirit. He could not bear to repeat exactly what was being said, and indeed, I should not want to hear such hateful slander!"

"Oh, dear," murmured Arabella. She had not thought ahead quite this far and saw too late that enlisting Sir Hampton's assistance would place her in the position of actually defending Sir James, or else betraying her hand too soon. Fortunately, Ellen did not require much in the way of words at the moment. She rattled on in great agitation, twisting a hapless scrap of lace between her fingers while Arabella held her and patted her back.

"I cannot believe I never saw until now what a dreadful, small-minded place this is. I have lived here all my life and never considered that there must be *some* places in the world where one is not forced to exist in a state of constant scrutiny and gossip," Ellen exclaimed, a scowl marring her pretty features.

"Perhaps there are—if one does not mind traveling to a place that is entirely unpopulated," Arabella said gently. With a rising sense of alarm, she saw how Sir Randall had twisted things to lead into his own goal of removing Ellen to the Continent.

"Such an existence would be preferable, I do believe," said Ellen with unaccustomed bitterness. "When Sir James first began telling me how he has always dreamed of traveling and living abroad, I confess that I was rather unenthusiastic at the thought of leaving home. But now I do not feel so opposed after all."

"Perish the thought!" exclaimed Arabella, doing her best to laugh as if she thought Ellen were in jest. "Of course, we cannot exist without you here, dearest. Putting aside how devastated *I* should be, imagine how bereft your poor parents would feel without you nearby. You are all they have, you know."

"I suppose that is true," Ellen admitted with some reluctance. She was already deeply tangled in Sir Randall's spell, Arabella thought, if such a thought had not already occurred to what had always been the most considerate and dutiful of daughters. "It was always a great sorrow for them that they were not blessed with more children. Mama, in particular, would be sorely grieved. She has mentioned several times in the past few weeks how much she is looking forward to seeing our family grow."

"I have no doubt that a man who loves you as ardently as Sir James does would never ask you to seriously consider removing yourself from your family if doing so would cause you any pain. It seems far more likely to me that he was only speaking in an abstract sort of way, you know," Arabella said diplomatically as she rescued the scrap of lace from Ellen's hands and smoothed it out on her own lap.

"That is quite possible. It would be lovely to travel once we are wed, of course, but not permanently. I daresay that once we are well and truly married the people around here will find something else to discuss," Ellen decided, brightening at the thought enough to offer Arabella a rather watery smile.

"They always do," laughed Arabella. "In that vein, why don't you tell me about your opinion on these lace samples. Unless, that is, you would rather destroy them all?"

"I have made a sad mess of this one, and yet it is still exquisite. I must have something utterly divine for the new traveling costume that is being made."

"Well, naturally! Nothing less than divine will do, dearest," Arabella said brightly, her true feelings masked perfectly.

PART IV

CHAPTER 20

Hurrying home from a clandestine meeting with Lord Willingham the next evening, Arabella was entirely preoccupied with thoughts of frustration. She had made very little progress in getting Sir Randall to tell her anything of his childhood, his reticence stemming less from suspicion, she thought, than from the overall foul mood which had taken hold of the man ever since Sir Hampton had begun his less than subtle assault.

Lord Willingham, likewise, had had precious little progress to report, his agent in the Ton meeting with a series of oddly reluctant interviews, and several dead ends. Literally. Which made Arabella worry all the more about Sir Hampton. Had she truly put the old man's life in danger? All in all, Arabella considered, there was very little actual progress that they could lay claim to, and she knew that time was drawing ever shorter. Sir Randall had mentioned once in her own hearing that he could scarcely stand to wait for the nuptials another heartbeat, and Arabella knew that he was not speaking in romantic hyperbole. She expressed her chagrin to Lord Willingham, who soothed her with promises that his contact in London was good at his job, and some notice would be coming forthwith. They only had to stay the course.

"But when?" she had cried. The lack of progress was frankly exasperating, and the weather was getting cooler. It was clear that they would not be able to continue meeting at the dovecote much longer.

"Soon," he had said taking her gloved hands in a most reassuring way. "Soon," he said again, and she closed her eyes as she leaned against his warmth. He put his arms around her. He was so very solid and imposing. She never felt that this plan was all going to fall to dust when she was with him. She believed she could save her friend and that Sir Randall's villainy would be brought to light. A spate of shivering went through her. Whether it was the cool wind, the fear of Sir Randall, or the momentary comfort in Lord Willingham arms, she was not sure. She only knew she did not want to leave that circle of warmth, just yet.

"You should go back," Lord Willingham said, pulling her bonnet closer around her face and tying it more snugly over her blowing strands of hair. "It is getting cooler with evening, and it will not do for you to be out and about unchaperoned as the day progresses."

"Yes," she agreed looking at the clouds which were casting a gloom on the late afternoon. "It must be nearly tea time."

"Perhaps I will have news from London with tomorrow's post," Lord Willingham said. "We must be patient."

Lady Arabella nodded and took her leave.

※

THE LACK OF PROGRESS WAS DISAPPOINTING, AND THE temporary reassurance and comfort that Arabella had found while conversing with Lord Willingham had evaporated almost the instant that she left his presence. It had been, she supposed, a transient sort of respite due to the relief of being able to speak openly. She smiled a little, unconsciously, as she made haste towards her home, thinking of something that Lord Willingham had said before she left. He always made her feel better. A slight smile graced her lips.

"Arabella Sedgewick, where in the blazes have you been these past two hours?" the earl's voice, unaccustomedly loud and stern, startled her badly. He seemed to have materialized out of nowhere, she thought, or else she had been so mentally abstracted that she had failed to see his approach.

"Father! You gave me a start," she exclaimed, clumsily attempting to stall for time. She had given a reasonable excuse for her absence before she went to meet with Lord Willingham, but for the life of her, she could not recall what the particular excuse had been.

"I shall give you a great deal worse than a start, young lady, if you do not give me an answer this instant. *Where* have you been?" her father boomed relentlessly.

"I've been… I was just… out walking," she finished lamely, quailing under his furious, fiery gaze. There had never been a time in her entire recollection that Lord Ashbury had been this angry with her, and the sensation was terribly confusing.

"Yes indeed, *out walking* with the only person whom I have expressly forbidden you to associate, isn't that correct?"

"What?" Arabella asked helplessly, feeling a shamed color rising to her face. All her years of endless efforts to keep from causing her father any distress seemed to have evaporated at once.

"Do you mean to deny to me—to my face—that you have been with that scoundrel, Lord Willingham, this very afternoon?" he demanded irately, and Arabella was so shocked at his knowledge that she could not quite manage to formulate any sort of denial. In fact, she had never outright lied to her father and did not think to do so now. She was at her heart a truthful person, and even lying to that relentless gossip, Mrs. Fillmore, was a stretch for her.

"I do not deny it," she murmured, unable to meet her father's furious gaze.

"I suppose I ought to think better of you for your honesty now, but as you have only told the truth once you were already found out I cannot say that I feel disposed to do so. Imagine my shock, Arabella, when I received a vicious, anonymous little note today, informing me that my oldest daughter has been keeping *unchaperoned* company with the worst fortune-hunter and rake that could possibly be found in Northwickshire."

"That's not true," Arabella burst out.

Father raised an eyebrow.

"I mean, he's not," Arabella said in a barely audible voice.

"Yes, well. I assured myself that such a rumor was patently untrue. I told myself. There couldn't be even the slightest chance that my Arabella, the model of decorum and propriety, would ever entertain such a notion. Would ever find herself in the company of such a rogue, and if she did by some accident, she would immediately excuse herself. I was sure, you would tell me of any impropriety."

"There was none…"

"I was perfectly ready to hunt down the author of that note and inform them of my great disgust for such low, unseemly machinations," he continued, the volume of his voice increasing.

"Father, I am sure that you are too angry and wounded to accept my apology," Arabella began, tears in her eyes, but Lord Ashbury cut her off without a moment of hesitation.

"Far from being able to accept your apology, I am not even able to *hear* your apology, young lady," He snapped. "A fine fool I would have made of myself, storming about the village, hunting down some anonymous letter writer, fueled by righteous, and entirely unfounded, as it turns out, indignation. I only stayed my impulse because I wanted to ask you if you might have any notion as to who would send me such a vile accusation."

"I believe I do have a notion as to that," Arabella said, half to herself as with a sinking heart she thought of Mrs. Filmore. She supposed that she had known all along that the woman's fragile sense of importance would not allow to insult of Lady Gatwick's ball to pass unrepaid. It had been foolishly short-sighted of Lord Willingham to insist otherwise, but then, she imagined it was in a strong man's nature to underestimate the vindictive abilities those who were weaker. Women such as Mrs. Filmore learned young to fight with innuendo and gossip which was as deadly as any sword.

"*That* hardly matters to me any longer, as that person was after all showing me a courtesy and consideration that my own beloved child could not be bothered with. When I could not readily find you, I asked your sisters if they had any idea of your whereabouts, and Daphne very helpfully supposed that you might be meeting at the dovecote with your friend who is so knowledgeable about restoring old buildings. I must say, Arabella, out of all the things I did not imagine you capable of, bringing your impressionable little sister into your scandalous doings is the very last possibility I would think to entertain."

"Indeed, Father, I did not intentionally bring Daphne in-" Arabella attempted another explanation but was once more rebuffed by her irate parent.

"Enough! I am far too furious to listen to your excuses and justifications. I will not hear another word from you, Arabella Sedgewick, for quite some time. This situation is quite without precedent, and I will say that I have not had time to reflect upon the best way to address it. At present, you may consider yourself as confined to your chambers, and you are to have absolutely no correspondence of any sort. Kindly do me the courtesy of proceeding there this instant," said Lord Ashbury in tones of steel.

It occurred to Arabella to attempt to argue with her father, but after only the briefest of hesitations she complied with his order in meek silence. He was angry, rightfully so, she could acknowledge that even as she smarted at his harsh tone. He was far too furious to listen reasonably to a tale which he would in likelihood have dismissed in the most equitable of moods.

She would simply have to hope that his outrage would give way before Sir Randall made his move. She could see no other recourse for the moment but retreat, although it rankled bitterly to be locked away in such obvious disgrace like a misbehaving child. Never had the earl even given Daphne such a punishment, even when it was well merited.

"Arabella? Are you awake?" Marianne's whisper, hours and hours later, was so soft that it barely reached Arabella's ears. If she *had* been asleep, it would certainly not have wakened her, but any sort of rest had proved to be patently out of the question. Frustration and inactivity had combined to keep her pacing her chamber floor well into the night, while both the tray of tea and dinner that had been sent up, remained completely untouched.

"Yes, I am," she replied softly. The door opened slowly to reveal Marianne and Daphne huddled together uncertainly, Daphne's eyes showing unmistakable traces of tempestuous weeping.

"Arabella, you must believe how terribly sorry I am, really you must!" exclaimed Daphne, flinging herself at Arabella. "I did not mean to get you into trouble. You must believe me." She hugged her sister fiercely, as Marianne stood in the doorway.

"Hush, of course I believe you, but you had better keep your voice down," Arabella admonished, pulling Marianne the rest of the way into the room and gesturing Daphne to settle in on the bed. "There is no sense in making Father angry with the pair of you as well."

"Father did not expressly forbid us to speak with you," said Marianne calmly as she took a seat by the mirror and turned the chair to face Arabella. "Although I daresay he would have if he had thought of it. I cannot say that I have ever seen him quite so discomposed in my entire life. You certainly meant what you said when you once decided to stop accommodating the needs and wishes of everyone else so entirely as has been your habit."

"I can assure you that I never intentionally set out to do *any* of the things I have done these past few weeks," replied Arabella wearily as she straightened the covers around her legs. "I am very nearly as surprised at myself as the rest of you are."

"I really, truly did not mean to give away your secret, Arabella. I did not realize that it *was* a secret," Daphne said insistently, as if determined to convince her sister and herself at the same time.

"Of course, you didn't, dearest, I do not blame you at all. It is entirely my own fault for keeping secrets."

"And you intend to persist even now in keeping them, don't you?" observed Marianne shrewdly.

"I fear I must, Marianne, but I beg of you, please do not be cross with me. It is not for my own sake that that I am keeping my own counsel, but for another."

"I believe you, but that is hardly going to stop me from asking questions since I am all but dying of curiosity. If you cannot answer them that is well and fine, but I expect you to answer anything that you are able."

"Certainly, and I can hardly wonder at your curiosity," Arabella agreed, smiling fondly at both of her sisters. "What would you like to know?"

"Are you in love with Lord Willingham?" blurted Daphne.

"What? In love with him?" Arabella repeated stupidly, sitting down on the edge of her bed as a strange and sudden weakness seemed to overtake her. Sir Hampton had asked the same question. No. He made the same assumption, and being the logical woman she was, she had to consider. Was she in love with Lord Willingham?

"I am asking about your own feelings, Arabella, not asking you to betray anyone else's confidence. He is a very handsome gentleman, after all," Marianne pointed out gently, moving from the vanity and sitting beside her on the bed.

"*Very* handsome," agreed Daphne with a mischievous giggle. "Don't you think he is handsome, Arabella?"

"You did just promise to answer us honestly where you could," prompted Marianne.

"I can honestly tell you…" Arabella trailed off; her thoughts suddenly unclear. There was no reason that she could think of to refuse to answer either question, but she felt a great reluctance to do so.

"Answer Daphne's question first, it is by far the easier query of the two."

"Well, I suppose I would say yes, then, I do believe Lord Willingham is quite handsome," Arabella admitted, a blush rising to her cheeks.

"Quite so. And are you in love with him?"

"Marianne, you are relentless, and the truth of the matter is that I simply do not *know*. I never even thought of such a thing until this very moment—well, until the question was raised," she amended thinking of Sir Hampton's assumptions. "But honesty compels me to confess that the idea has struck me with great force."

"Oh, how wonderful," Daphne breathed rapturously. "Bella loves the baron."

"I said no such thing," Arabella protested sharply. "I only said that I do not *know*."

"Which is precisely how we can see that you are in love," explained Marianne kindly, as if to a small child. "You have always known when you were *not* in love with someone, so the very fact that you cannot identify your feelings is a great clue, I should think. I *am* pleased."

"Pleased? What madness are you speaking now?" demanded Arabella, baffled. "You cannot mean that you are pleased to think I *might* be in love with a person our father despises; a man with whom Father has forbidden me to associate?"

"Oh, I have no doubt that you will overcome such trivial obstacles as those," laughed Marianne with a wave of her hand. "And I am positively delighted to see that you have fallen in love after all and not foolishly sacrificed yourself by marrying some dull, suitable creature out of a ridiculous sense of duty. Come along, Daphne, we had better not risk Father's wrath by staying any longer," she added briskly, rising.

"Father *did* say that we are not to carry any notes from or to you," said Daphne, giving Arabella a cheerful embrace. "But I shan't let a trifle like that stop me if you want to get a message to Lord Willingham."

"Quite so," agreed Marianne. "But it will have to wait until tomorrow evening, I believe, for Father has ordered us to accompany him to Morelane first thing in the morning. He apparently has some unavoidable business to attend to there. I fancy he thinks we will aid and abet you somehow if we are all three left unattended here for most of the day. He is quite right, of course. In the meantime, it won't do you any good to starve yourself to death, you know. Eat a few bites of your supper." She paused a hand going to the cooling teapot. She grimaced. "I shall have a fresh tray sent up," Marianne said. "Then eat while it is hot, and try to get a little rest."

"I will try," Arabella agreed meekly. It was most unusual and disorienting to be put in the position of being tended to by her younger sisters, but she could see the sense in what Marianne said all the same.

CHAPTER 21

Lord Willingham wandered restlessly around the work crew that was, for a change, laboring industriously about his stable renovation. Other work must have been difficult to come by that morning, he thought cynically, but he would gladly accept the novel sight of many strong hands building up the crumbling walls of the building.

Or, rather, he *ought* to be glad, but instead, he found himself unable to either enjoy the spectacle or pitch in to contribute to it. All morning long he had been unable to shake a definite sense of wrongness, as if things were coming to a crisis point. Nothing had changed whatsoever, as far as he could tell, yet the feeling that something was amiss positively dogged him. It was foolish, he told himself in vain, and besides, there was nothing he could actually *do* at the moment.

He and Lady Arabella had been pressing their luck a bit too far lately, and Mrs. Filmore's discovery of them together brought home how easily he could compromise Lady Arabella. While he could think of nothing better than being constrained to marry the beautiful Bella, it hardly seemed fair to her. Doubtless once they had managed to save Miss Millworth and cast out James Randall, Lady Arabella would marry one of the fortunate, blameless suitors who panted constantly after her.

The thought filled Lord Willingham with enough wrath that he was forced to channel it into his work, and he labored alongside the workers until he had succeeded in driving all thoughts of her out of his mind. Almost.

ARABELLA SAT CURLED UP BY HER BEDCHAMBER window, drowsing slightly over a worn book. She had certainly not managed to sleep for even five minutes together the night before, and the weary night had finally caught up with her as the morning hummed quietly along. Sleep, indeed! She thought with a faint shake of her head. Between the intense concern and distress for Ellen which had been her constant companion for weeks, her guilt over upsetting her father, and frustration at being confined to her chambers like an errant child, it had been a sleepless night. Besides worrying about Randall, she had Mrs. Filmore's spitefulness with which to contend. It was just too much.

How much more profound had her wakefulness been, once, compounding all of those factors, Marianne had persisted in asking that dratted, ridiculous question! *Did* she love Lord Willingham? The idea had nagged at her relentlessly, refusing to be put to rest. Marianne had suggested that her very uncertainty provided the answer, but Arabella was not so certain. Surely when someone was in love they knew it, didn't they?

Arabella realized with an intense burst of annoyance that her first inclination was to talk the matter over thoroughly with Lord Willingham himself, as it was, he, with whom she had become so thoroughly accustomed to discussing her problems. That, of course, would hardly be possible in *this* scenario, she thought, although it was slightly amusing to picture what his reaction would be if she broached such a topic.

"Oh, thank you for meeting with me on such short notice, Lord Willingham. This dovecote is truly a romantic and picturesque spot, is it not? My sisters thoroughly think so. A perfect place for a tryst." She considered waving her hand about the dust and cobwebs. Laughing she said the words aloud, amused with herself and confident that there was no one nearby to hear her foolishness. "I have asked you here because I wish to discuss a matter of importance and your counsel is positively invaluable to me, you know. No, no, nothing to do with the imminent destruction of my dearest and oldest friend's happiness. That has proved quite beyond my abilities, I fear. Sir Randall or whoever the wretch may be is certain to win his foul little game here. No, Lord Willingham, I want to ask you if you think that I have fallen in love with you, since *I* certainly do not know the answer. I know absolutely nothing any longer, to tell you the truth, but I feel you can enlighten me."

Closing her eyes and laughing softly, Arabella imagined the man's reaction. His eyebrows would certainly quirk up on that endearing way that they had, and his blue eyes would darken to that stormy gray that was his particular shade. He would study her from his great height with that look of puzzled and annoyed admiration that always set her heart beating just the tiniest bit faster. And then he would say…

Drifting off to sleep in spite of her interesting daydream, Arabella's thoughts tangled themselves with true dreams, which somehow shifted into portentous-seeming nightmares. She was not looking up at Lord Willingham, but at Sir Randall, and he was not smiling quizzically, but rather snarling with such venom that she recoiled even in sleep.

It was as though his carefully curated mask of charm and respectability had finally slipped away and she was able to see his true nature glaring loathsomely at her in her dream. Too late, she thought pointlessly, she was seeing the truth too late, and his cold hands gripped her arms painfully as he raged and raved and shook her. They stood on the church steps, and she knew, in the way of dreams, that they had just been wed. Her hands were not her own, she realized, but Ellen's, and the lovely little gold band that she had been so proud to receive only moments before was tightening around her finger painfully. She struggled to free herself from Sir Randall's grasp so that she might attempt to remove the ring, yet try as she might she was trapped and helpless.

Tears rained down her face, but that only seemed to enrage Sir Randall even further. He was dragging her away, somewhere, and all the while the gold band was cutting inexorably into her finger. Blood welled up around the gold band and she thought the ring would cut straight through to bone.

Arabella jolted suddenly awake with a gasp that was very nearly a shriek. She could never recall having such a vivid, horrifying dream before in her life—indeed, her ring finger ached painfully in spite of the fact that there was nothing actually constricting it. The stress of the past few weeks, compounded by her sudden confinement and sleepless night, she thought, must have finally been too much for her strained nerves.

Her body was twisted in the bedsheet and she was covered in sweat, but Sir Randall was nowhere in sight. Her hand, which was hanging down towards the floor had fallen asleep. She rubbed it gingerly, glad that there was no rabid ring upon it to vex her. It was rather warm in the room; she thought as she got up to open the bedchamber window and see if the autumn breezes had persisted.

She pushed back the draperies and glanced out of her window; her gaze attracted by some slight movement on the grounds below even as she rubbed at her weary eyes. Catching sight of a carriage rattling hastily down a generally unused side road that wound past the Sedgewick estate, towards the North Road, she shifted to look more closely at the sight. The driver, heavily cloaked despite the mild autumn weather, was urging the horses onwards rather mercilessly, she noted. It was really quite odd to see someone in their quiet neighborhood traveling with such evident urgency in the middle of the morning, and her curiosity was piqued in spite of her exhaustion.

As the carriage rumbled around a bend in the side road, Arabella was wracking her mind to think if she could recognize it from any particular estate, but it was quite unfamiliar. The slender arm, swathed in a delicate pink sleeve, however, was nearly as familiar to Arabella as her own. Ellen had been showing her a new dress for her trousseau only two days previously, made with fabric of that precise shade, Arabella was certain. She gasped.

What appeared to be a handkerchief fluttered to the ground, evidently released by the passenger, and the arm withdrew once more into the carriage as it thundered out of sight.

It *had* been Ellen, Arabella was utterly confident, and she had very deliberately thrown her handkerchief from the carriage just as she was hurtling past the Sedgwick estate. Ellen had mentioned no plans of going anywhere, certainly not in such extreme haste, and Arabella could only conclude—spurred perhaps by some lingering urgency from her dream—that her friend was in dire trouble.

"And here I have been so foolish and careless as to get myself confined to my room right at the moment when she needs me the most," Arabella exclaimed to herself, leaping from her seat beside the window.

LADY ARABELLA AND THE BARON

There was no question, unfortunately, of her making the same sort of daring escape out of the window as Lord Willingham had done the night of Lady Gatwick's ball. Arabella's bedchamber was three stories high, and there were no convenient vines or neighboring ledges. Hindered by her skirts, such a climb would be suicide.

She was at least not actually locked in her chamber, the earl evidently trusting either her or their staff enough to not have felt that such a precaution was warranted. Really, Arabella thought with a wry smile, he ought to have known better on both counts. If she was so far removed from her ordinary, well-behaved habits as to meet with scandalous gentlemen unchaperoned, then she would hardly quail at slipping out of the house even if she had been ordered to stay within.

And as for the servants, well, who knew their whereabouts and schedules better than she did herself? Arabella was confident that she could avoid every member of the staff with relative ease, particularly at this time of day, when a great deal of the household would be sitting down to their own breakfast in the servant's hall.

She started to hasten to her doorway, but then thought better of it. Whatever her feelings towards Lord Willingham might or might not be, she could be certain that he was the person she was most able to depend upon in a moment of crisis. She paused long enough to scribble a quick note on a scrap of paper, and then slipped out of her bedchamber door.

CHAPTER 22

Stealing as noiselessly as she could down the heavily carpeted passageways, Arabella made her way through the enormous manor. She was nearly frantic to get to the handkerchief that Ellen had thrown from the carriage, but she made two quick detours first, one to her father's study to take up an antique dueling pistol from his collection displayed there, and then to the kitchen gardens where she knew that one of the stable hands routinely kept a tryst with the pretty parlor maid after morning tea. She had always pretended not to notice, considering the housekeeper's rules about flirtations betwixt the staff to be rather too heavy-handed to be reasonable. It was one thing to keep decency and decorum in place, but quite another to forbid the poor girls from ever so much as speaking to their beaus.

"Good day William, Anne," she said briskly, rounding a corner of the border hedge and startling the pair badly.

"Lady Arabella!" gasped poor Anne, her face changing rapidly from bright red to pale white, then settling on a delicate shade of green. "Oh, Lady Arabella, begging your pardon-"

"Never mind about that," Arabella interrupted, not unkindly. "If I minded the two of you meeting here occasionally, I should have put a stop to such goings-on when they began last Michaelmas."

"It was nothing scandalous, Lady Arabella. Indeed, Anne and I should like to be married—" offered William, his broad face flaming with embarrassment at the very word.

"I am aware of that as well, William, and you certainly have my blessing, but I really do not have time to spare on this just now. I'm in a dreadful hurry and I daresay you know that I'm supposed to remain in my chambers."

"His Lordship did mention something to that effect," William admitted reluctantly, looking more embarrassed than ever.

"Unfortunately, I am unable to abide by those orders at the present moment," Arabella said coolly. "I am also unable to comply with my father's command prohibiting my sending or receiving notes, and I will require your assistance in that, I am afraid."

"Oh well, really, Lady Arabella, our orders were terribly clear," began William apologetically, but Arabella cut him off with a sorrowful shake of her head.

"It won't do, you know, William. I hate to point this out, but I believe your orders regarding fraternizing with the household staff were quite clear as well."

"That's so, William," Anne agreed hastily, putting a hand on her beau's arm, and giving him a pointed look.

"Ah, well, yes, I suppose I see your point, Lady Arabella," he stammered after a moment's pause that had Arabella fairly gnashing her teeth with impatience.

"I am delighted that you do. I thought you might come around to my perspective. You must make all possible haste now. Saddle my mare and bring her to the bend in the side road, I will meet you there. And then you must take this note to Lord Willingham over at Willowbend Farm and insist upon delivering it to his hands and his alone. Is that all perfectly clear?"

"Er, yes, of course, Lady Arabella. Right away, then."

"Marvelous," Arabella replied, thrusting her note into his hands and barely sparing Anne a smile and nod before turning to hurry towards the spot where Ellen had thrown out the handkerchief. The pistol was a heavy, nerve-wracking weight in her reticule as she ran, and doubtless she would have no need of such a thing, but there was something reassuring about its unfamiliar presence, nevertheless.

So great was her haste that it took Arabella a few moments of frantic searching before she was able to locate Ellen's handkerchief—trampled in the dust of the road. Shaking it clean and smoothing it out as best she could, Arabella could definitely see that not only did it definitely belong to Ellen, but also that the word 'help' was hastily scrawled on the delicate linen fabric.

Whatever could that villain Sir Randall be doing, she wondered helplessly. Could he actually mean to abscond with Ellen against her will?

"Here's your horse, milady," William announced with breathless triumph, evidently having decided to enter into the spirit of the thing and embrace his role as co-conspirator. "I do believe I've just set a record for speed, for never was a horse saddled quite so quickly in times of peace."

"I daresay you are right," Arabella said, doing her best to give the man a smile of approval despite the fear and urgency that threatened to consume her. "Please help me up, William, and then do your best to set another record in getting my note to Lord Willingham."

"Yes, Lady Arabella," he agreed and helped her quickly into her saddle. "Will that be everything that you need, then?"

"I believe so—no, wait. Give this handkerchief to Lord Willingham as well and tell him that I saw it being thrown from the carriage," Arabella decided.

"Which carriage?"

"My note to Lord Willingham explains it. Don't trouble yourself with that, but you may tell him precisely where I found it and show him the exact location if he asks. Make all possible haste, William," she added urgently. "It is terribly important, you know.

Actual *lives* may be at stake here, and I am relying upon you."

"You can count on me, Lady Arabella," William replied fervently. He might have said more, but Arabella could restrain her impatience no longer and whatever his further words were, they were lost as she spurred her mount onward.

It was very rare—indeed, Arabella could not think of a time before when it had occurred—for her to push her horse into a full gallop, but she did so without a second thought. So much time had passed since she had seen the carriage, and at the rate it had been traveling they would be miles and miles beyond her already.

Never had their small community witnessed such a sight as the perfect and proper Lady Arabella Sedgewick all but flying on horseback, her bonnet hanging by its strings and her pale gold hair coming loose from its restraining coif to stream wildly behind her. Doubtless any who saw her thought they were experiencing a hallucination, but Arabella did not so much as spare them—or her formerly pristine reputation—a fleeting thought. There was no space in her mind for anything besides the sole idea of catching up with the carriage.

When Arabella came to a crossroads she was forced to rein in her horse, who although unused to such reckless riding from her, seemed to be enjoying the race. In vain, she looked about for some helpful farmer or passing traveler who might have seen the carriage pass and be able to tell her which road it had taken, but the crossroad was utterly deserted as far as the eye could see.

"If the scoundrel means to marry Ellen legally, I imagine he would take her to Gretna Green, but how can he imagine he will get anyone, even in the wilds of Scotland, to agree to unite a man to an obviously unwilling bride?" she mused, and then scolded herself for such short- sighted thinking. Sir James Randall, the impostor, would find threatening and intimidating Ellen into keeping her peace almost as simple a matter as he would find it to fool an unwitting blacksmith priest, and two witnesses. No doubt money would secure the witnesses, and since he was after Ellen's fortune, he would consider the payment of the witnesses an investment. He must surely intend to marry her, Arabella thought. At least, that meant he would probably not ravish her on the road.

With a sound of disgust, Arabella turned her horse's head towards the North Road which led most directly towards Gretna Green. Unfortunately, that place was at least a full day's journey hence by coach, perhaps more. Would they press on, or stop at an inn? Either option would be Ellen's ruination. Arabella thought fleetingly of how sore and weary she herself would be after such a long and arduous ride on horseback, but that was no matter. Her friend was in peril. She could do nothing less.

Arabella considered tossing one of her gloves on the road as an added precaution so that Lord Willingham might find it and know which way she had gone, but she needed her gloves. Without them, the rough leather of the reins would cut into her soft hands, and in time she would have blisters. She could not afford to be so handi- capped in her riding. Instead, she slipped a finger under the ties of her bonnet and pulled it from her head. The sun on her face was the least of her worries. A moment was spent remembering Lord Willingham tying this very bonnet. Surely, he too would remember. She flung it onto the road a few feet onto the path she would take. Then she leaned forward and urged her horse once more into a furious gallop. Her hair came loose from its final pins and trailed out behind her like a silvery halo.

"Lord Willingham, sir?" Christopher glanced up, blinking sweat out of his eyes, to see an unfamiliar and decidedly disheveled servant approaching him.

"Yes?"

"I'm William Conley, sir, one of the stable hands over at Ashbrooke Manor? I have a message for Lord Willingham—a most urgent message from Lady Arabella Sedgewick, but I am only to deliver it to his lordship's hands, no other. Please take me to him," the young man said uncertainly, giving Christopher a rather skeptical look.

He did not strike a very lordly appearance just then, Christopher realized, with his shirtsleeves rolled up and mud thickly caking his boots.

"I am he. I can assure you of my identity; indeed, if you prefer to examine documents establishing the same, I shall be all too happy to oblige, but you did mention that your message is most urgent, didn't you?" he prompted the man.

"Oh! Yes, terribly urgent. That's all right then, if you are indeed—well, here is the note, and Lady Arabella asked me to give you this handkerchief as well."

Christopher felt his blood turn to ice in his veins as he scanned the contents of the brief note. It was bad enough that Randall had absconded with the hapless Miss Millhouse, the very thing they had been working so diligently to prevent, but for Lady Arabella to have gone off in reckless pursuit of the pair! He could imagine only too well a variety of evils that might befall her before he was able to find her.

Unceremoniously shoving both the note and the rather mangled handkerchief back into William's hands, Christopher said,

"How much time has passed since Lady Arabella left?"

"Not a full quarter of an hour, my lord, if you can believe me. Lady Arabella said as this was a matter of life and death, and I made as much haste as I possibly could, seeing as how I could tell she was in real earnest," answered William soberly.

"I do believe you, and you have done well. I have no time to lose now, so you must take this note from Lady Arabella and give it to Lord Ashbury, explaining everything that has happened this morning."

"But the earl is in Morelane for the day," William protested, evidently not relishing the idea of making such a delivery. "And he will be terribly displeased to hear that I've been aiding and abetting Lady Arabella today—I don't know as what she's done to cross him, for generally speaking it's she who runs the household and has for years, but the earl has ordered her to remain in her chambers and all the staff was told not to deliver any messages to or from her ladyship."

"What on earth would make the man do such a thing?" Christopher wondered rhetorically, then shook the question aside even as William began to protest that as a stable hand, he was not privy to such knowledge. "Never mind that, it hardly matters now. Listen, William Conley, a great deal is at stake here. I do not think that Lord Ashbury will be angry when all is said and done, but if he is vexed with you due to your involvement in this, I promise that you will have a place here at Willowbend. I shall be in need of good, dependable staff presently. But you *must* ride out to Morelane with all haste and give Lady Arabella's note to her father without another moment's delay, do you understand?"

"I do, and I will. And I thank you, sir," William replied stoutly, already leaping back into his saddle as Christopher strode away.

CHAPTER 23

Arabella had imagined that she would have to ride for hours and hours, perhaps even into the night, before she could have a hope of catching up with the carriage. Resigned to that weary prospect, she was taken by surprise when after only an hour and a half she spotted a carriage pulled alongside the road ahead of her.

She knew riders on horseback generally traveled faster than a coach, but she had not credited it, especially traveling side saddle.

Slowing her horse cautiously, she felt about in her reticule for the heavy handle of the dueling pistol. She hadn't the slightest idea of how to use the thing—or even if it were loaded, which she rather doubted—but Sir James Randall had no way of knowing either of those things. For all *he* knew she was an expert shot, she told herself, attempting to bolster her courage as she approached the pair.

The carriage sat quietly amid the grassy roadside, no sign of movement from within. Sir Randall was busied with one of the horses, his heavy overcoat flung carelessly aside. It was most definitely he; Arabella saw with some relief. Aside from the urgency of finding the man, she had no desire to accidentally accost a stranger at gunpoint, but Sir Randall, she would happily shoot for his villainy.

Guiding her horse off of the road to walk quietly alongside the grassy bank, she made her way as silently as possible to Sir Randall, her approach going unnoticed as the man cursed furiously about horses and horseshoes and farriers—and the entirety of the world along with them, from what she could tell.

When a branch broke beneath Arabella's horse's foot and Sir Randall looked up, finally aware of her presence, he found himself looking straight into the muzzle of her firearm.

"I will shoot you if you so much as take a single step," Arabella cautioned the man as firmly as she was able.

"Why, Lady Arabella, such a violent sentiment!" mocked Sir Randall, straightening from his work slowly and putting his hands up. "I'm sure you do not want to shoot me."

"On the contrary, I will do so," Arabella said, eyes flashing with menace as she steadied her horse.

"Such an extraordinary appearance," he said with irritating calm. "You look something like a cross between an avenging Valkyrie and an irate fishwife. I doubt anyone of your acquaintance could imagine such a sight." Arabella's horse stepped forward towards the trees and a delicious patch of clover that grew there.

"My appearance is hardly any of your concern," Arabella returned haughtily as she attempted to keep her horse engaged and the pistol aimed. "Although my violent sentiment certainly is. I mean what I say, Sir Randall—or whoever you really are. I will not hesitate to shoot you if you do not release my friend at once."

"Arabella?" Ellen's voice called out, slightly muffled, from within the carriage.

"I am here, dearest."

"Yes, *dearest*, your champion has come to save you from my clutches," scoffed Sir Randall. "And what a champion! You never did care for me, did you Lady Arabella? And now you have uncovered my secret, I see. This will never do, you know."

With a lightning-fast movement, Sir Randall kicked up a scattering of gravel at Arabella's horse, while at the same instant pivoting out of the line of her pistol. Her horse shied in reaction, twisting and leaping to the left. Arabella, unfortunately lost her balance as the horse practically jumped from beneath her. She fell from the saddle. The pistol fell beyond her reach.

"Ah, yes, that will be quite enough of that nonsense," Sir Randall snapped, dropping even the mockery of a semblance of charm from his manner as he snatched up the pistol and aimed it at Arabella. "Get up! Now, on your feet."

"You will not get away with this," Arabella snarled as she struggled to rise, her feet entangled in her long skirts. She did not think that she was badly hurt from the fall, but it was difficult to tell, with her nerves singing so frantically.

"On the contrary, *Lady* Arabella," her opponent scoffed. "I am getting away with it. Perhaps, I have one hostage more than I originally intended, but I am quite adept at improvising when needs must. You may have the great honor of accompanying myself and my fair bride on our nuptial trip to Gretna Green. Into the carriage with you now."

"I should rather be shot in the road like a dog than go anywhere with a hideous scoundrel such as *you*," Arabella retorted scornfully, summoning a bravado that she in no way felt.

"That may very well be arranged, madame, if you insist upon delaying my plans any further!"

"Sir James, no, I implore you!" Ellen's tearful shriek cut through the air as she flung herself from the carriage to stand beside Arabella. Sir Randall fired the weapon which clicked empty.

He laughed. "You accosted me with an unloaded weapon?" he asked, but Ellen was appalled.

"You would have shot her?" she cried. "You would have shot my friend?"

"Get back into the carriage, Ellen," Sir Randall snapped, swinging the pistol around to point it at his fiancé.

Although the gun was only valuable as a bludgeon, Arabella knew that there would be no sense in reasoning with the man. He clearly was possessed of not even a solitary shred of human decency. He would have shot her where she stood if the gun had been loaded. Arabella doubted he had much more empathy for Ellen.

"Come, Ellen, I will be with you now," Arabella said soothingly, laying a hand on her friend's arm. The two made their way, unassisted, into the carriage, with Sir Randall watching their every movement.

"That's right, it is so nice to see that you can be made to understand reason, Lady Arabella," he said with a leer. "And just think, if only your father had had the courtesy to cut your trip to Bath shorter by a few weeks, *you* might be in the admirable position of being my fiancé rather than Ellen here."

"Do not flatter yourself, sir," Arabella replied coldly. "I was not taken in by your false charms for even a moment."

"Ah, but you would have been; I assure you. There has never been yet a young lady who managed to resist me when I once set my sights upon her. Indeed, I toyed with the idea of making you fall in love with me regardless, Lady Arabella. It would have been so interesting, playing upon the affections of two such close friends, pitting you against one another as rivals. If I had more time for the game, I assure you, I would have led you both on a merry chase."

"Why?" Arabella cried. "Why would you do such a thing?"

He shrugged. "Why not?" he said.

"You are a monster," sobbed Ellen, cringing behind Arabella as though she could not bear the sight or sound of her former beloved.

"What an uncharitable term, especially coming from a young lady who only yesterday termed me 'the most wonderful gentleman who ever walked the earth.' Very fickle, Miss Millworth, very fickle indeed," Sir Randall mocked her tears relentlessly. "I ask you, is that any way to speak of your future husband?"

"I will *never* marry you," Ellen gasped out in a valiant attempt at defiance that nevertheless evoked a laugh from Sir Randall.

"Certainly, you will, my dear. And you father will hand over your dowry and then some, and you and I shall away to the Continent. Who knows, if you amuse me, I may even allow you to provide me with an heir or two before some unfortunate accident befalls you."

"Sir James, you cannot be so cruel, I won't believe it of you even now," protested Ellen. "You cannot be so cold-hearted and unfeeling as to casually speak of such things."

"Ah, but I can be, my dear," laughed Sir Randall callously, and the sound made Arabella's blood run cold. "That shall be your first lesson as my wife, I do believe. Others, far wiser and more knowledgeable about the world than yourself have failed to learn that lesson, though, so I do not have terribly high hopes for you. Your friend Lady Arabella here, she does not fully comprehend my nature. She has nothing but a blind sort of instinct, I believe. Her instinct was correct, as it turns out, but *so* difficult to prove. And her friend and ally, the disgraced Lord Willingham? He ought to know, far better than most, what I am capable of, yet even he has been hamstrung by his own concept of morality. Even now he perceives only a fraction of my true capabilities."

"I wonder what you can mean by such a statement, sir," said Arabella in tones of icy contempt. "Lord Willingham certainly knows the great evil of which you are capable. He has told me himself such stories as would surely consign you to eternal perdition."

"I can assure you that he knows only a portion of my wicked deeds, my lady. If he knew the whole, why there is simply no way that he might remain even as barely civil as he has been these past few weeks."

"What do you mean by that?" Arabella demanded, leaning from the carriage, her curiosity piqued in spite of her anger and fear.

"Only that Lord Willingham, if he were but clever enough to know it, owes his current impecunious state to me, my dear Lady Arabella. In addition to Miss Millworth's dowry, you know, I have the greater bulk of poor, sad Lord Willingham's fortune in my possession or very nearly. It is safe with a friend of mine on the Continent, awaiting only my arrival.

"The late, unlamented Lord Willingham, you may have heard, was a terrible fool—a gambler and a spendthrift. Well, I daresay you know what they say about a fool and his money? They are easily parted and all that. It was very nearly child's play to part old Lord Willingham from *his* money, hardly worthy of my own particular talents, really. A murmured suggestion here, a forged signature there, and the unfortunate baron was penniless and indebted before he knew what had happened, and why would his heir expect to find anything other than debts and disgrace when his reputation was so thoroughly soiled.

"A rather tidy crime, for all its simplicity. Really, I must say, absconding with the object of Willingham's affection as well as his fortune is quite poetic. I wonder, now, perhaps I really ought to marry *you* after all, Lady Arabella," he said as he began to climb into the carriage. "Your father is sure to pay handsomely to keep your family's honor intact, I daresay, and there would be some satisfaction in—"

"That is quite enough of that," cut in a very welcome voice suddenly, and to Arabella's shock Sir Randall collapsed, crumpling to the ground, and revealing the figure of Lord Willingham standing behind him.

"Lord Willingham," Arabella gasped, relief and surprise making her feel weak all over. "You are versed in fisticuffs," she said amazed.

"Yes, well," he said, dropping the stone that he still held in his hand. "I thought I should have some insurance that

I would not need a second blow, although carrying a rock in one's fist, is not really sporting."

"I do not care how sporting you were," Lady Arabella pronounced, leaping into his arms. "Sir Randall is anything but sporting. However, I must say, what marvelous timing. You received my message, then?"

"I may never recover from the shock of that message, Lady Arabella," Lord Willingham said gravely as he took her into his arms, kissing her quite thoroughly even with Miss Millford as a witness, murmuring against her hair, my Bella.

She had not at all recovered, when he continued speaking. "And I may be so bold as to suppose that your poor stable hand will not recover any time soon either, as I did him the further discourtesy of sending him to inform your father of the days' goings on; since, I did not feel that I could spare another moment in coming to your rescue, Lady Arabella."

She noted the recovery of his lapse in etiquette, and was not sure she wanted to go back to such formality. She wanted to melt into his arms. "I am very glad you did," she said.

"Poor Father may never recover, either, for that matter," Arabella reflected. "I daresay that I have cancelled out a dozen years' worth of good behavior in one single day as far as he is concerned."

"Arabella, can you ever forgive me?" cried Ellen.

"Of course, I forgive you," Arabella said. "There is nothing to forgive."

"But I have been such a terrible fool. I think, there was never any greater fool in all the world," sobbed Ellen. She paused, looking at Sir James. "Is he dead?" she asked peering at the man who lay unceremoniously on the ground.

"He is not dead," Lord Willingham assured her. "He will recover, if you are alarmed on that account. I did not kill him, you know, I simply could not forbear to hear him say such vile things for even a moment more."

"It wouldn't be any great loss if you *had* killed the wretch," observed Arabella, and she realized with some alarm that she meant her words quite literally. "That sounds dreadful, I am sure, but there was never a more sinister man. If you will forgive me, Ellen; it is such a relief to finally speak my true opinion of him."

"Society would certainly not mourn the loss of such as he," agreed Lord Willingham.

"Society, nor myself either," Ellen managed, attempting with great effort to stay her tears. She covered her face in shame. "I am such a fool."

"He has fooled many others, I assure you," Lord Willingham said.

"He is a heartless monster," Arabella added.

"Oh, do not think that I am upset on his account," Ellen said. "But all the same I *do* mourn a loss. I mourn for the man I believed I knew and loved. That man is quite dead, along with any feelings I might have had for the wretch. When he pointed the gun at you, Arabella. I could not—" She burst into tears. The next words spilling out in an incoherent rush. "He would have shot Arabella if she had brought a loaded pistol."

"There now, dearest," murmured Arabella, embracing her friend soothingly as the girl sobbed.

"Pistol?" Lord Willingham said in confusion.

"I brought my father's pistol," Arabella admitted. "But I had no idea how to load it or fire it. In fact—" She looked around on the ground for the item, but Lord Willingham picked it up before she could recover herself enough to grasp it.

"Are you quite mad?" he asked.

"Perhaps just a little," Arabella said. "I thought I could frighten him. I guess that was foolish. I do wish I knew how to shoot. We were quite defenseless until you arrived, Lord Willingham. It is not a good feeling for a woman to have."

"But you should not attempt to fire a gun if you are not proficient in its use," Lord Willingham said. "Since, I do not think I shall be able to prevent you from flying to the rescue of those you love, I think that is a lack that should be remedied. I do not ever want you to be at such risk again."

"What do you mean?" Arabella asked thinking that it was not his purview to teach her how to shoot…unless…

He shook his head as he glanced at Ellen who was still crying. "I'm getting ahead of myself," Lord Willingham said, looking rather distressed at the prospect of a more detailed conversation with a hysterical woman on the side of the road. "There will be time enough to discuss the matter later. Allow me to assist you both back into the carriage, ladies. Then, I will bind this scoundrel up and place him beside myself up front, so you need not gaze upon him another moment."

"One of the horses went lame," Ellen said as he helped her alight. "That is what slowed our journey."

"Thank Providence for that," Arabella added.

"All of these horses have been badly used, I fear," Lord Willingham said as he examined them. "But I think I can get this shoe righted, at least temporarily. Nonetheless, our return journey will be rather slow. I will have you both safely home, eventually."

"Thank goodness for you, Lord Willingham," Arabella said softly as she allowed the gentleman to take her hand and assist her into the carriage. Then, he went to collect her startled mare, who having found a patch of clover, was contentedly grazing through her bit at the roadside.

CHAPTER 24

Much later, Arabella and Ellen were comfortably installed in Ellen's chambers, and being tended to by a baffled Mrs. Millworth while the gentlemen discussed recent events, quite volubly. Arabella's father and sisters had only just arrived along with the local authorities.

"The magistrate has arrived," Marianne announced briskly, returning to the room from an errand they had invented to give her the opportunity to discover what was happening since the gentlemen had ushered the woman from the room with admonitions of the conversation was much to distressing for the ladies.

"These ladies have just lived through those distressing events," added Daphne in a huff and Arabella hugged her youngest sister for her solidarity.

"And Lord Willingham's friend from the Ton," Marianne said. "Arrived with that very handsome Doctor Roger

Larkin. I imagine he will be along presently to tend to you, Ellen."

"I did not know he was so young when Father was complaining of him," Daphne added. "I thought all doctors were old and crotchety."

"I don't believe I need a doctor," Ellen protested, her voice a little hoarse from crying. "I am not really hurt anywhere, just a sore on my arm where…"

"Where that beast nearly wrenched your arm off," Arabella finished savagely when Ellen trailed off in distress. The print of Sir Randall's hand stood out in a livid bruise on Ellen's pale, soft upper arm.

"Arabella, please. Do not fuss," Ellen said. "I am alright."

"My poor, sweet darling," Mrs. Millworth said, brushing through Ellen's disordered hair as if she were a little child. Arabella suspected the activity was as much for her own benefit as for Ellen's. Arabella had never seen the calm, cheerful Mrs. Millworth so distressed as when they had brought Ellen to her.

"I thought you were lost to me," she whispered as both she and her daughter hugged each other among much tears. "You must know you mean everything to me." Ellen winced at the tight hug and her mother examined the bruise.

"I daresay I deserve as much, or worse, for being such a great fool," Ellen sighed. "But it *was* terrible, all the same. The change that came over him so suddenly was astonishing, as though he had been replaced by a different person altogether."

"Can you bear to tell us what happened?" wondered Arabella gently.

"I think I must. He came upon me when I was walking in the garden and began speaking of how impatient he was for us to begin our lives together; how the wedding day could not come soon enough to suit him. He often spoke like that, you know, I thought it was terribly romantic. But then he became quite urgent, and said we must not delay another instant, that it was a crime against Love itself to squander the time we had been given. I did not really comprehend what he meant, not at first, so I said that perhaps we could convince Mama and Papa to move the ceremony up a few weeks, although it would be rather difficult. There were so many preparations to make. He said no, it was a matter of moments, not weeks, and that we must be married this very day, we must run away together at once."

"He must have realized that he could not keep up his charade much longer," Arabella reflected, sipping the tea that Marianne pressed upon her. "Whether it was due to Sir Hampton's questioning or the inquiries that Lord Willingham's agent was making I cannot say, but either way I fear I am to blame for this."

"I will not hear such nonsense, Arabella," Mrs. Millworth said firmly. "If it were not for your actions, that criminal would still have us all fooled. They might have been to Gretna Green by now." The woman shuddered with the thought.

"I knew he was dangerous, but I did not anticipate he would resort to actually kidnapping," admitted Arabella.

"Probably he did not think it would come to that," said Ellen. "I—it is so shameful to have to admit, but I considered running away with him willingly. It seemed so thrilling and passionate, you know, to be loved so ardently. But then I thought of how much distress and scandal such a thing would cause my family, and it seemed too selfish. I am sorry I thought of it for even a moment, Mama." She turned back to Arabella as her mother patted her back gently. "When I said as much to Sir Randall and made him believe I was truly in earnest, that I would not leave with him for Gretna Green, I think he lost his head. Truly I do. He said such vile, hateful things to me. I will not repeat them, but suffice it to say that he made his contempt for me quite clear. He said he had no more time or patience to spare on the ridiculous sensibilities of a silly girl, and that we were to be married that very day and I was to cooperate or else be ruined. Before I could fairly grasp what was happening, he placed his hand over my mouth to prevent me from screaming and dragged me to his waiting carriage."

"My poor darling, I cannot bear that such a thing has happened to you, and right under my very nose," said Mrs. Millworth, tears slipping silently down her cheeks as she listened to her daughter's woeful recitation. "I shall never forgive myself for missing the signs. Parents are supposed to protect their children from such things."

"It isn't your fault, Mama," Ellen protested, turning to press her face to her mother's shoulder, comforting them both. Arabella felt a momentary pang, wishing for perhaps the thousandth time for her own mother, for anyone to comfort her thus. She barely remembered her own mother's face, much less her holding and comforting her as a child. This, if anything, she realized, was what she envied Ellen, not her suitor, but her family, and the deep abiding love that was shared between them. No matter what else happened in the world around them, they had each other and their love.

"The scoundrel fooled a great many people, both here and in London," Marianne pointed out. "It was just his poor luck, I suppose, to come up against my sister, Arabella Sedgewick." She beamed at Arabella, and for a moment, Arabella was exceedingly grateful for her own family. She did not have a mother, but she had sisters who did indeed love her, and although Father was not demonstrative, she knew, deep in her heart, that he also cared for her. In his own way, that was why he had locked her away from Lord Willingham, to keep her safe. It seemed all so far away now that everyone was home safely.

"How *did* you know he was not all he seemed to be?" Ellen wondered, turning to her friend. "I am forever grateful that you did, of course, but what was it that made you see his true nature when no one else could?"

"I hardly know," admitted Arabella. "Something about him just struck me as false right away. I think he must have suspected that I knew, too, for he was ever on his guard with me. He would not look me straight in the eye. He just seemed oily; I suppose.

"I saw none of that in him," Ellen said. "He was a perfect gentleman."

"I know, dearest, but he was on guard with you. With me, I think he had a different plan; to separate me from you, and to separate you from all who loved you. I feared that a straightforward approach on my part would have caused him to alienate us altogether, and indeed, there was very little I could say to *prove* my suspicions to you. After all, they were only suspicions. I hope you can forgive me for not being more forthcoming."

"Only if you can forgive *me* for being such an easily led little fool," Ellen said, a note of bitterness in her voice. Arabella wondered how long it would take to undo the damage that Sir Randall's deception had done to her friend's sense of self-worth. That mark, she feared, would linger far longer than any bruise.

"Doctor Larkin is here for Miss Millworth," a maid announced, tapping at the door and slipping inconspicuously into the room.

"Of course, show him right in," answered Mrs. Millworth quickly, rising from her seat at Ellen's side.

"We probably ought to go speak to Father, Marianne," said Arabella, thinking to give her friend some privacy. "I daresay he has quite exhausted his patience in wanting a more detailed explanation of my actions."

"Lady Arabella, the earl suggested that you might be unwell yourself," Dr Larkin said, entering the room. He was a quiet, steady man—handsome enough, as Marianne had said, but always a little careworn and untidy looking. His deep blue eyes showed traces of distress, Arabella thought, as they glanced from her face to Ellen's.

"There is nothing whatsoever the matter with me, I assure you, sir. I am rather tired, and perhaps a bit sore from such an unaccustomedly long ride, but a good night's rest is all the cure I could possibly require."

"If you are quite certain, then? Your father was concerned over your welfare," he replied, but when Arabella repeated she was well, his gaze turned once more to Ellen with some anxiety.

"Come along, Arabella. We shall leave Ellen to be ministered to, and hopefully Father will have the sense to let you rest a little before he scolds too much," said Marianne, darting a curious look at the doctor, who had evidently forgotten them already in his eagerness to aid his patient.

Leaning gratefully on her younger sister, for she really was quite sore from the long and frantic ride, Arabella made her way down the stairs and to the parlor where the various gentlemen were assembled. She was braced for an onslaught of recriminations, but to her surprise her father took her immediately into his arms and embraced her.

"My dear, brave child, thank goodness you are unharmed," the earl said, in a voice thick with emotion. That, more than anything else that had occurred all day, made tears spring unbidden to Arabella's eyes. "I find myself to be equally terrified and proud at hearing what you have been involved in these past few weeks. You are so very, very like your mother, you know, my dear."

"I am so, so terribly sorry, Father, for causing you distress," she whispered, hugging him back. "It was not my intention, I assure you, but it was wrong of me to act so recklessly. I must beg your forgiveness."

"Nay, child, your actions were noble, and I have only myself to blame that you were unable to confide your concerns to me. I have apologized to Lord Willingham for my prejudiced and unwarranted attitude towards him, which I have no doubt is the reason that you felt the need to act in secret."

Arabella drew herself up a little, pulling from some unknown reserve of strength. "I would like to say, Father, that Lord Willingham has behaved in every possible way as a gentleman, and I believe most sincerely that his reputation is quite unfounded," Arabella said, surprised by her father's attitude but not wanting to lose an opportunity to repay Lord Willingham's kindness towards her. "Any impropriety in our friendship was in the interest of helping Ellen, and indeed, it was all at my own behest."

"There, child, I do not think ill of Lord Willingham. As I have just been telling him, I was shocked as when poor William came racing up to me with a very garbled version of events. I will confess that I felt quite murderous until I was able to ascertain your safety and well-being, but knowing everything that has taken place, I am content that nothing untoward has happened. We all owe Lord Willingham a great debt of gratitude for his actions in revealing that scoundrel Randall, as well as our sincere apologies for our treatment of him heretofore."

"It has been my pleasure, Lord Ashbury," said Lord Willingham with a somewhat stiff and formal bow. "And indeed, it has been to my benefit to oust the wretch, for evidently a great deal of my inheritance is in his possession and may actually be recovered. I never would have dreamed such a thing possible. My Uncle John had assumed that he lost the money fairly."

"All is well that ends well, you see?" Lord Ashbury exclaimed grandly, before Arabella could respond to Lord Willingham. It was for the best, she supposed, as she had no idea what she would have said. After the intensity of the past days, she felt suddenly awkward and foolish in his presence. "But Arabella, I do beg of you to leave off having such dramatic episodes for some time. It isn't fair of me to expect unexpected behavior only from Daphne, but you must ease into these things in the future—I am not a young man, after all." He chuckled somewhat at his own joke, but Arabella knew the truth of the matter. Her father was the only parent she had, and he was up in years.

"Of course, Father," Arabella murmured meekly. Her eyes met Lord Willingham's and his answering smile warmed her spirits for a moment before she was bundled off towards home.

CHAPTER 25

A fortnight later Arabella stood in the doorway of the old dovecote, a shawl drawn snugly around her shoulders against the faint chill of the autumn afternoon. The old structure was to be restored in actuality; Daphne having refused to let go of the idea even though she understood it had simply been a convenient excuse that Arabella had invented. Of course, Daphne's whims must be acted upon. Arabella smiled at the thought.

What was more, it was to be reinstated to its original purpose as a dovecote, the earl having agreed that his late wife would have liked the thought of her daughters thinking of her when they heard the birds call.

It was wonderful, really, Arabella thought with a smile playing around her lips, the change that had come over their family in the past weeks. The shock of discovering that she was capable of both defying her father's wishes and rescuing her friend had made Lord Ashbury realize, so he had said, that he was not quite the well-informed and involved parent he had imagined himself to be. His increased interest in his daughters had done wonders already for Daphne's behavior, and therefore for everyone's peace of mind. Perhaps, it would have taken nothing less than a near- catastrophe to bring about such a dramatic and needed change, Arabella supposed.

Ellen, although her nerves had suffered a terrible shock, was recovering nicely, aided by the devoted care of her parents and the dedicated Dr. Larkin. It would take some time, surely, to mend the damage that Sir Randall, or rather, Mr. James Tyner, as the man's true name was discovered to be, had done, and they were all still reeling with what a narrow escape she had managed.

The little town was still humming with the scandal, of course, with everyone eager to insist that they had mistrusted that scoundrel all along. Sir Hampton, the only person to have established his suspicions before everything came to a head, was regarded with a livelier terror than ever. He seemed to be decidedly enjoying his status as an excellent judge of character.

Everything had worked out beautifully, Arabella reflected, and yet her satisfaction was undeniably bittersweet. She would not deny to herself that the cause lay in the direction of Willowbend Farm. Lord Willingham had accompanied the magistrate in escorting Mr. Tyner back to the authorities in London and had remained there to recover his inheritance. Arabella had had a brief and rather businesslike note from him upon his arrival, informing her that the villain had been put on a vessel bound for the penal colony, but she had heard nothing from him since.

Doubtless, she had been very foolish and romantic herself, falling in love with the man she had dragged unwillingly into such a chaotic situation, and imagining that he might feel anything other than relief once he was rid of her, she thought with a sigh. It was precisely the sort of thing she would have scolded Ellen or Marianne for considering, and yet, she could not deny that she *was* in love with Lord Willingham.

Everything about him was so dear, she reflected, with his ingrained gallantry disguised so perfectly by his rather blunt and straightforward manner. She adored his exasperated smiles, and his unwavering assistance, and the steadfast way he soldiered on despite circumstances or public opinion. No, she would not deny that she was hopelessly in love with him, and none of her acceptable suitors could even begin to compare with him.

It was horribly ironic, she supposed, to find that she *was* capable of falling ardently in love, but only with a man who was unlikely to ever see her again. The lands of his barony were somewhat further south. Doubtless with his fortune restored, and a barony to update, Lord Willingham would not waste his time on a little, out of the way, Willowbend Farm, and Arabella would have no way of convincing him to fall in love with her.

That, she realized, was exactly what she must do. She certainly could not stand the idea of marrying any of the insipid young gentleman she had been considering, and the idea of sitting idly by while Lord Willingham went on with his life and perhaps married some other girl! It was insupportable, she decided although pursuing a man and convincing him to fall in love with her was hardly proper or ladylike. Arabella had discovered recently that it did not do to *always* behave decorously. Perhaps young Daphne had the right of it. One should follow their passion, whatever or whomever that might be. She took a deep fortifying breath.

Her mind made up, she turned away from the dovecote with a determined scowl, thinking a little distractedly of Lord Willingham marrying someone else. To her utter surprise, the gentleman in question was standing not four paces away, regarding her with that familiar quirk in his brow.

"Lord Willingham! You startled me, sir," she gasped, blushing as if he could read her thoughts.

"My apologies, Lady Arabella. And ought I add, my sympathies to whoever has caused you annoyance, for it looks to me as if you were quite vexed."

"You may keep your sympathies for yourself," Arabella tossed back, rather neatly, she thought. "I am surprised to see you here, that is all. I thought you would have a great deal of business in Town."

"I have, and I will have for quite some time, I fear, but I could not do without attending to some urgent business here first."

"Regarding Willowbend?" asked Arabella, her heart sinking. Really, he shouldn't have been able to sell the place so quickly, as small and neglected as it was.

Without the remaining tie of the farm, she could not fathom how she might contrive to be near enough to the man to make him fall in love with her.

"In part, yes. I have just been finalizing my purchase of the adjacent lands on the northern side of the property," Lord Willingham replied, looking at her searchingly.

"You—you purchased land? Arabella faltered, confused.

"Not only land, but a house and outbuildings. You are familiar with Wellington Abby?"

She opened her mouth and closed it again. Wellington Abbey was indeed the neighboring estate, but it dwarfed little Willowbend Farm. It was nearly as large as her father's estate, although not a part of an entail. It had once been an Abbey, but had been empty since Lord Noxingham moved to his London townhouse after the death of his son in the war.

"I thought you were going to sell Willowbend altogether," Arabella said.

"Whatever would have given you that idea? I have always meant to restore and enlarge Willowbend, it is just a much simpler matter now that I have recovered my inheritance. I have a great affection for the place, you know. Besides, the fact that the land here might actually support the gutted barony, I like the neighborhood." His smile was wide and knowing. She was not sure what to make of his glee.

"I did not realize, but... that is welcome news, I suppose."

"Well, I am glad to hear you say so, for otherwise I might be a trifle discouraged regarding the rest of my business here," Lord Willingham said, smiling as he took a step nearer. "You see, I've just been speaking with your father, explaining to him that it really would be best for you to marry me. For one thing, our names *are* linked rather scandalously. For another, it so happens I'm madly in love with you."

"Oh!"

Lord Willingham took her hands most tenderly in his, and smiled at her, the passion in his eyes making his intentions clear. "I have been for quite some time now." He reached up to tuck a stray hair under her bonnet, but then changed his mind and pulled the strings of her bonnet, loosening it and letting it fall back from her head. Her hair slipped inexorably from its pins, but she did not care. He took the bonnet from her head entirely and her carefully coifed hair cascaded down her back without the aid of the bonnet holding it in place.

Lord Willingham buried his face in her silken hair. "I have longed to do this for weeks," he said.

She tipped her face up. "What?" she asked.

"This," he said, and he put two fingers beneath her chin and kissed her.

Arabella had never thought that a kiss could so transport a soul. She felt her toes curl in her slippers as she stood on tip toe to get closer to this man she loved. Yes, she most certainly loved Lord Willingham. The whole world seemed to burst into color, as a rosy heat filled her breast with passion and with love. The scent of autumn and sandalwood cologne filled her nostrils as Christopher's hands traveled up through her hair. He held her close, murmuring, "my Bella." It was a very intimate gesture since she had not given him leave to call her by her given name. On the other hand, she had not given him leave to kiss her, but she would not take that moment back for the world. She wanted many such moments with this man. Her Lord Willingham. Her Christopher.

Finally, he breathed a ragged breath against her neck. "I thought I lost you," he said. "Never had I felt so bereft. I lost all of my fortune and my lands. I lost everything I held dear, and yet nothing compared to the moment of devastation that I felt when I thought I lost you, my dearest, my only, beautiful, Bella. Say you will marry me."

She nodded gingerly, too overcome with emotion to speak.

"I spoke to your father," he said, "I asked for your hand."

And Arabella at last found her voice. "I hope, for Father's sake, that he agreed with you," Arabella said, her heart soaring at his touch on her cheeks, her lips, her hair. "for I had just been determining to myself that I was going to make you fall in love with me. I really cannot bear the idea of marrying anyone else."

"Had you? I almost regret not being able to give you the chance to do so, Lady Arabella, for it would promise to be quite amusing. However, I am forced to confess that I have loved you practically since the moment you ran me to ground and demanded that I help you save your friend. You are, you know, the most breathtaking and enchanting creature, and not just for your ethereal beauty, but for your courage and your loyalty to friends. For speaking your mind and doing what you think is right."

"Stop," she said laughing.

"Do you love me, then?" He rubbed a thumb across her lips, causing her to shiver with delight. "Say that you love me, my Bella."

"I certainly do." She laughed, Arabella tilted her face up to meet his lips softly, thrillingly, in a kiss that seemed to stop time itself.

Many moments later, as a chilly wind accosted them, Arabella lay her hands on his chest. She could feel the steady thrum of his heart beat. She did not want to part from him, but one day soon she would not have to do so. The thought filled her with bliss. Still, she knew they could not stay cloistered at the dovecote as much as she loved the time alone with him. She smiled up at him and said, "We should share our news with my sisters."

"And mine," Lord Willingham said replacing her bonnet with alacrity. "I want to invite my Aunt Jenny to bring them to stay at Willington Abbey for Christmas, although I am a bit frightened at what will happen when Lady Daphne and my sister Lydia join forces." His eyes were alight with happiness, and she could not wait to meet his family.

"Oh yes," Arabella said with a laugh. "I remember you said you had sisters. I shall be happy to meet them."

The sudden feeling of family was delightful, but most of all, this man, this wonderful man was to be her most intimate family—her husband. As they turned towards the house, hand in hand, she looked out on the splash of autumn color that graced the countryside. At last, she had found her true love, and she thought, all was right with her world. She could not be happier.

COMING SOON

To continue reading Miss Millworth's story

NEXT BOOK IN THE SEDGEWICK LADIES SERIES

M iss Ellen Millworth paused for a single moment in the dim foyer of her home, taking the time to fix a careful smile upon her face. Her parents, she knew, would immediately and unconsciously search her expression the moment they set eyes upon her, and she would not for worlds cause them distress by showing anything but a pleasant smile. She could not recall a time in her life before where she had needed to school her expression into a smile – indeed, according to family lore she had been smiling almost since the moment of her birth.

But these last few months had brought on a great many new and unpleasant experiences to her door, and having to order herself to smile was hardly the worst of her trials, she supposed.

"Oh, there you are darling, back from your visit with Arabella already?" Her mother, Mrs. Millworth exclaimed, rising hastily the moment that Ellen stepped into the cozy parlor. "I had thought that you meant to spend the entire afternoon with the Sedgewicks."

"We had a lovely visit, Mama, but had to cut it short because the Earl was called away unexpectedly and needed Arabella to entertain some visitors of his," Ellen explained, taking a seat near the one her mother had just vacated. "Marianne offered to keep them occupied, but Arabella is far too kind to allow her to suffer all afternoon, knowing how Marianne despises small talk."

"Poor Marianne may as well start becoming accustomed to entertaining Lord Sedgewick's visitors now. The task will fall to her as soon as Arabella and Lord Willingham are married," Mrs. Millworth observed, in the indulgent tone in which she always spoke of the Sedgewick sisters. "Although I daresay that Arabella thinks to spare her as long as she can. I know she has resolved to stop shielding everyone from unpleasantness, but it's quite the long-standing habit with her, isn't it?"

"I rather think it is more than a habit, for it seems to me to be a part of her very character," Ellen agreed, smiling genuinely at the thought of her cousin and dearest friend, who had a tendency to shoulder the weight of the world as a matter of course. "Fortunately, I believe that Lord Willingham will help her find a sort of balance in that sort of thing. He adores her so; it is difficult for him to stand by idly and watch her put herself last."

"He is a dear boy, if I may be allowed to refer to a grown, to say nothing of titled, man in such a manner. I am constantly delighted that those two have found one another. How are preparations coming along for…" Mrs. Millworth suddenly trailed off, looking stricken. It was due to the fact that she had been about to mention the upcoming wedding between Lady Arabella Sedgewick and Lord Christopher Willingham, Ellen knew.

"Mama, really, I hope I am not so delicate that I cannot bear to hear the word 'wedding'," Ellen said with a small amount of asperity. "You know how happy I am for Arabella, and so does she."

"Of course, my darling, of course I know that. I only hate to say anything that might cause you any distress. You know that Doctor Larkin cautioned your father and I against reminding you of… recent events, at least until your unpleasant dreams cease to have such strength and frequency."

"I slept quite well last night, Mama," argued Ellen stubbornly. "Like a baby, in fact."

"You never cried in your sleep as a baby," Mrs. Millworth pointed out quietly, looking at her daughter with a steady gaze that was piercing despite its gentleness.

"I do not want you to have to be so constantly concerned over my state of mind, Mama," Ellen said, moving closer to her mother, and wrapping her arms around her thin shoulders. Mrs. Millworth had never been inclined to frailty, and Ellen realized that worry over her only daughter's troubles had been affecting the woman even more than she had realized.

COMING SOON:

Click the link to join my VIP Readers and be notified when this book is published.

Want Even More Regency Romance…

Follow Isabella Thorne on BookBub
https://www.bookbub.com/profile/isabella-thorne

❧

Sign up for my VIP Reader List!
at
https://isabellathorne.com/

Receive weekly updates from Isabella and an Exclusive Free Story

❧

Like Isabella Thorne on Facebook
https://www.facebook.com/isabellathorneauthor/

SNEAK PEEK

~.~

Continue reading for a SNEAK PEEK of:

The Forbidden Valentine ~ Lady Eleanor Hawthorne

THE FORBIDDEN VALENTINE

Snow flurried down around Lady Eleanor Hawthorne. It clung to her eyelashes, her stylish hat and her fur cloak. Eleanor's boots were made of the finest smooth leather, but they were somewhat slippery and not very warm. She was up to her shins in snow as well, standing beside the sleigh with one arm wrapped around herself, and the other holding the draft horse's head. Her poor elderly driver, Arthur, was down on his knees in the stuff, his grey head bowed as he sought to deduce the problem.

With his head beneath the sleigh, the driver's words were muffled. "One of the stanchions is cracked, Lady Eleanor. Rotten luck, that. Had them checked before the season and there was not a hint of rot on 'em." He sat back on his heels, and doffed his hat. "I am terribly sorry, but I cannot see it making it back to Sweetbriar in this state. If it cracks clean through..." He let the thought hang. "I am sorry, Milady."

"It is not your fault in the slightest," Eleanor said. "You could not have seen that rock, buried under all this snow, and it is just a lucky thing old Mouse here did not stumble over it and hurt himself." She rubbed the horse's shaggy nose and he lipped at her glove, looking for treats. She edged closer to the horse, borrowing his heat in the cold wind.

Arthur got to his feet and brushed snow from his trousers. He rolled his hat in his hands. "I might walk back to the Albemarles' residence and secure a means of repair, but that does not solve anything, as I cannot be leaving you out in this weather with naught but a horse for protection."

The weather was nothing more than a snow flurry at present, but to Arthur any amount of risk was too much for Eleanor. She peered up the road the other way. It was difficult to see through the haze of falling snow in the low, failing light, but there was a hazy golden glow upon the hilltop, less than half a mile's distance.

"What of that house?" Eleanor asked. She gestured towards it.

Arthur shook his head and yanked his cap back on over his head. His ears were rimmed a bright red. "I could not go there, Milady. That is the Firthley House, as you well know."

Lady Eleanor sighed and stamped her boots, trying to bring some life back to her frozen feet. She slipped slightly in the wet snow and clutched onto the horse's mane to steady herself. The big gelding turned his head to look past his blinkers at her, and then stood stoically in the cold.

Eleanor's boots, like her clothing was quite fashionable, but the boots lacked the fur lining to make them warm enough for the weather and the new leather soles were treacherously slippery. What had begun as a pleasant day of shopping in town had turned rather difficult. Her packages sat neatly boxed in the back of the sleigh, covered by canvas. She, however, was becoming quickly covered by snow.

"Yes, I do know it is Firthley Manor," Eleanor said, "But I think under these exceptional circumstances, it may be reasonable to disregard the absurd feud of our families and ask for some assistance. I am certain they would lend a hand to a lady stranded in the snow. We are practically neighbors, after all," said Eleanor.

She was referring; of course, to the feud between the Hawthornes and the Firthleys that had existed since before she was born. The original cause for the argument had never been adequately explained to her. Eleanor suspected the reason for that was because neither of her parents actually remembered what had begun the whole affair, but were too stubborn to admit their ignorance. The feud had caused the odd tension in the local circles. Hawthornes would not attend, nor be invited to, events hosted by the Firthleys, and vice versa, and they did their best to avoid meeting at the social gatherings hosted by other members of society when they could. From everything Eleanor had heard, and she had asked about, the Firthleys were a perfectly ordinary family much like her own, and no one she asked had the faintest clue what had started all of the nonsense; or if they did, they would not tell her.

"If your parents found out I asked at the Firthley house for aid…" Arthur tutted. He was clearly torn between finding help for Eleanor as swiftly as possible and earning the ire of her parents.

Eleanor, with sudden inspiration, proposed a compromise. "Well then you shall not ask at the Firthley house. I will. Here," she said, gesturing toward Mouse and passing Arthur the reins. "You take over this job and I shall find us some help."

This caused Arthur to turn as red as his ears. The loose, wrinkled skin at his neck trembled, but he came up beside her and took her spot at the horse's head.

"I do not think this is the best course of action, Milady" said Arthur, in a wavering voice. "Your parents will be livid."

"We shall not tell them, then. After all, they never speak to the Firthleys. How will they ever find out I went to their door? I shall be back as soon as possible, Arthur. Perhaps you should climb beneath the blanket and try your best to keep warm. I do believe the temperature is dropping with the sun, and all this slush will turn to ice." Before he could come up with any more arguments against the idea, Eleanor hurried off in the direction of the Firthley house.

Hurried was too generous a word. Even with the aisles of snow smoothed down by the passages of other sleighs, it was treacherous going in the middle of the road, and her boots were not equipped for such travel. The snow was deep enough at the side of the road that her boots sunk in, breaking through the top layer of frozen snow. That gave her an awkward gait, but at least the snowfall was not high enough to cover her boots, and the deeper snow actually gave her some footing in the slippery slush. However, the drifts along the side of the road were large enough to wet the hem of her dress and cloak.

By the time Eleanor reached the drive of Firthley Manor, she was warm from her exertion, and sweating in her layers of fur and wool, although her feet were still cold and the hem of her dress was sodden. She took a moment to straighten her clothing. Eleanor smoothed her hair back beneath her cap and brushed the snow from her shoulders with the back of her glove. It was the first time a Hawthorne would stand on the Firthleys' doorstep, in who knew how long, and she did not want to be the cause of a bad impression. Somewhat decent, but hardly looking like the lady of quality she was, Lady Eleanor Hawthorne marched up the drive and knocked at the door.

Eleanor waited. The sweat from her exertion began to dry, leaving her chilled and shivering. Just like that, all her warmth was gone. Her toes felt like hailstones in her boots. Eleanor knocked again. She could see a light in the entrance hall. Peering up at the house, one of the rooms above was also lit by what appeared to be a cheery fire, but there was no answer at the door. She huffed and knocked again. Briefly, she had the foolish notion that those within could somehow tell she was of the Hawthorne line, and were refusing to answer on principle. Of course that was absurd, she was so heavily bundled in winter clothing that it would be impossible to tell who she was unless they stood just in front of her. Still, no one answered.

Thinking of poor old Arthur, waiting and freezing at the sleigh, Eleanor turned to go. Arthur would say it was all for the best that they had not answered her and would they would be forced to walk back the way they had come; to the Albemarles' house, over a mile away. Eleanor shot a last, sullen look over her shoulder at the house, and picked her way down the front stair. The steps were treacherous with snow and ice and she clung to the railing.

"Oh, hello there," a voice called from somewhere off to the left. The sudden voice caught Eleanor by surprise, so that she did not see a patch of ice on the final step, directly beneath her foot. Her boot slipped and her feet shot out from under her. Eleanor lost her grip on the railing and landed quite indignantly on her bottom in the snow.

~.~

Continue reading about Lady Eleanor Hawthorne in
The Forbidden Valentine ~ Lady Eleanor Hawthorne

~.~

To find more Regency Romance stories, please visit
Isabella Thorne's Amazon Author Page

~.~

Would you like to be notified of new releases, special updates, and giveaways?

Sign up for my VIP Reader List!
And receive a FREE STORY just for joining

Printed in Great Britain
by Amazon